Take My Heart

SWEET HART INN ROMANCE

MADDIE JAMES

SAND DUNE BOOKS

Take My Heart

Maddie James

A Sweet Hart Inn Romance, Book 2

About Sweet Hart Inn

Welcome to Sweet Hart Inn... Where the kitchen is always warm and love is always on the menu.

Nestled on the peaceful edge of Falls Lake in the heart of the Blue Ridge Mountains, Sweet Hart Inn is more than a cozy bed and breakfast—it's a place where hearts heal, friendships form, and romance is served with a side of sass.

At the center of it all is Suzie Hart, a chef-turned-innkeeper whose recipes have a way of bringing people together (and finding their way into her books) —and sometimes, sparking unexpected love. Along with her (soon-to-be, maybe?) husband Brad, Suzie welcomes a delightful cast of characters through the inn's front doors, such as runaway brides, brooding bachelors, holiday guests, disgruntled daters, and more.

Whether you're looking for a heartwarming holiday escape, a second-chance romance, or a cozy story filled with culinary charm, the Sweet Hart Inn series delivers all the feel-good vibes you crave.

Bon appétit! And enjoy.

Take My Heart

A SWEET HART INN ROMANCE, BOOK 2

When Shelley Hart ran off and married her sister's fiancé, the whole town of Harbor Falls was in a twitter. A few years later, with her husband deceased and two little girls to take care of, Shelley realizes her only recourse is to go home.

The last thing Shelley Hart wants is to go home for the holidays. She left Harbor Falls years earlier and hasn't returned. Her leaving humiliated her entire family and caused friction with her older sister, Suzie. Who could blame Suzie for being upset? After all, Shelley ran off and married Suzie's fiancé, Cliff.

But everything has changed now—and going home is her only option.

Harbor Falls Police Officer Matt Branson values being alone, even during the holidays. Dubbed the town hermit, he prefers the solitude of his mountain cabin to socializing with friends—friends who say he still pines after the woman who got away. But the snowy day he pulls over an older model sedan speeding into Harbor Falls, things change. His gut slams against his backbone as a tearful woman rolls down the car window. His heart melts when she looks up into his eyes.

Shelley Hart is back in town—the woman who sent him into his cave in the first place.

Chapter One

"I can't believe I'm doing this."

Shelley Hart slammed down the trunk lid on her old Dodge Stratus and grimaced as the gas cap flew off and tumbled over the parking lot.

Darn thing. She stared as it rocked back and forth on the asphalt. The little door was sprung, and the cap never worked right after her tank got siphoned. The siphoning incident happened the first night she moved into her new apartment here in Dalton Springs, which occurred three months after the bank notified her they were taking the house, which took place six months after her husband had died.

Nine months. Long enough to have a baby.

No, thank you very much. One of hers was screaming from the backseat, already.

"Be there in a minute, sweet pea."

She glanced back at the apartment and frowned. She'd had high hopes she could make it on her own. Without Cliff. But no. Didn't seem to matter how far she tried to stretch the dollars, there were never enough. Her gaze lifted to the sky behind the complex. It was overcast and gray, tinged with a pink early evening sunset. A winter sky painted with cotton candy. The weatherman promised a white Christmas and the air smelled like snow.

The mountains rose in the distance, strong, sturdy, and secure.

"Harbor Falls is over there," she whispered. "Home...is over there."

Strong, sturdy, and secure. She supposed she needed that. She'd not had a strong shoulder to lean on since Cliff died—maybe it was time she leaned on family.

Her gaze played over the Blue Ridge Mountains. Only forty-two miles separated Dalton Springs from Harbor Falls—but a chasm of hurt and past indiscretions stood solidly in her way.

She swallowed hard and swiped at a tear with a gloved finger. Soon she'd have to swallow a whole lot more than spit. Pride. Yes, that was it. It had been nearly three years since she'd been home. The last thing her sister, Suzie, expected to see this Christmas was Shelley on her doorstep, homeless and penniless, with two little kids in tow—the ones she'd had with Suzie's fiancé, uh, *ex-fiancé*. Whatever....

Yes, she'd caused quite the small-town scandal. That disgrace even beat Polly Gruber running off with the preacher. Didn't seem to matter to anyone that she and Cliff were happy and loved each other. Oh, she knew the repercussions, running off with her sister's man. The whole town thought she was pond scum. Lower than pond scum, even.

But Suzie and Cliff were taking a break, officially, and Suzie had moved to Asheville for a while. And he was lonely.

Wasn't entirely her fault, was it?

One thing led to another and then—

Then they'd ran off and gotten married. Suzie found out later and all hell broke loose—in the family and in Harbor

Falls. And then Cliff had to go and die and leave her in this mess. No insurance. No savings account. No family.

No matter. Home was where she was heading. Home to Harbor Falls, and for the holidays, no less. With no plans ever to return to Dalton Springs—Dalton Springs and Cliff were all in the past.

Sniffling, she wiped another tear before it froze to her lashes.

Home. Harbor Falls.

She was about to suck it up and head home to family, like it or not.

Taking three brisk steps forward, she bent, snatched the gas cap off the blacktop and twisted it back into place on the car. She rounded the vehicle and got in, not looking back.

Just forward.

"Come on, girls," she said. "Let's see if we can fix this mess."

≈

A brisk gust of wind rocked the vehicle. Harbor Falls Police Officer, Matt Branson, turned up the heater and lowered the volume on the country music station on the radio. "Damn. Must be a helluva storm coming."

He pushed a few buttons to scan the stations, hoping to find something with a local weather report. Would be nice to know what he was in for tonight, sitting here on the side of the road waiting for unsuspecting speeders to dart by. Lucky for him, he was assigned the newest police cruiser the city of Harbor Falls, North Carolina owned. Nice vehicle, too. He did enjoy a perk now and then with his job. He liked to think it was because he was the only officer with a degree in law enforcement, but probably not. The other officers were homegrown and locally trained, but they were good ol' boys and did one helluva job.

Besides, it was Harbor Falls, right? The village force was small but reliable enough to handle anything that Harbor Falls threw at them. A domestic or two, a kid gone awry and of course, the speeders. Biggest trouble was the occasional tobacco smuggling, a few pot plants growing in the foothills, and once a homemade Meth lab run amok, but the county Sherriff's department and the regional ATF guys took over those, mostly. Harbor Falls was little more than a 21st century Mayberry, R.F.D.

He hoped he was a lot more than a modern-day Barney Fife.

He'd left town a year or so after high school—had pretty much fled with his head hanging and his heart on his sleeve, if he remembered it accurately—and in a few years had himself that degree from Eastern Kentucky University.

Damn proud of that, too. So was his Mama. Because of that degree, and the fact that he brought all that new-fangled knowledge back to his hometown of Harbor Falls, he was pretty much top dog cop in these parts. Well, not counting the Chief.

So here he was. Waiting.

Of course, it wasn't like he had a horde of family members at home. He probably wouldn't even see his Mama until tomorrow evening at the Methodist Church candlelight service, and his sisters were all due to arrive very late Christmas Eve night with a passel of his nieces and nephews. They wanted to be home in Harbor Falls on Christmas morning, much to the chagrin of their husbands.

Other than that, there was no one.

Frowning, he shifted in his seat, pushed that thought out of his head, and glanced out the window. Lucky for him, the east end wasn't the busy end of town. At least he wasn't walking the downtown beat sniffing out shoplifters. Lit up like a roman candle for about three weeks, the town of Harbor Falls eagerly welcomed the shoppers and they came in droves. All that marketing about Harbor Falls had paid off the past year or so. He had to admit it brought some mighty strange folk out of the hollers.

So, in a way, he was grateful not to be downtown. On the other hand, not a single car had ventured by in the last fifty-two minutes. The town council thought sitting out here was a wonderful idea. They needed revenue for the force, so they had passed a new ordinance lowering the speed limit in both directions. The guys on the west side were pulling them over right and left. He could hear that on his radio. The action on the east, however, was, well, non-existent.

Bored, he watched as small ice crystals formed in little pellets on his windshield. He let them pile up on his wipers and then swished them away. That kept him busy for about three minutes. He breathed on the window next to him and drew funny pictures on the glass, then smeared them off with a leftover fast-food napkin, leaving behind ghostly images. He upped the temperature and turned on the defroster to keep the fog down.

Should a speeder happen to venture by, it might be good if he could see out his window.

Finally, he reached under the seat, pulled out a piece of wood, and dug deep into his pocket for his whittling knife. Not eager to get shavings and wood chips all over his new cruiser, he laid the napkin out on the seat beside him and started to whittle.

There. Perhaps this wasn't so bad after all. He could sit here until the snow piled up and whittle, if he had to. Putting knife to wood was the one thing that kept him company for hours on end when he was at home—in his cave, as his sisters called it. He loved that cabin he'd built up on the mountains, though. Cave or not, it was his, and he had learned to be okay with how his life was turning out up there.

So okay, his social life sucked. He refused to call himself a hermit, although when not at work, he spent most of his time at home. Living a solitary life had both its advantages and disadvantages. Carving wood helped him keep his sanity.

Just didn't do a damn thing for keeping his bed warm at night.

His knife hand stilled on the wood and his head jerked up. A vehicle raced in from the south, popping over the hill. He reached to swipe away the fog from the driver's side window that failed to dissipate. The dark blue sedan whizzed by, and he quickly stashed his knife and wood under the seat.

"Hot damn."

Tucked back in the lane of the old Casey place, he pulled out from his hidey-hole and turned on his lights and siren.

∾

It wasn't like Harbor Falls was that far away from Dalton Springs, but in North Carolina, country roads aren't laid down in straight lines like they say a crow flies. Winding and narrow, the two-laner twisted through the foothills of the Blue Ridge Mountains. Mostly, Shelley took her time while the kids napped.

It was when she pulled into Village Grove that she made her mistake.

Even though the girls' tummies were full, she had not eaten herself since morning. Up early packing boxes, she'd scrambled a couple of eggs and then washed and packed her skillet. After that, eating hadn't been a priority. Figuring out what to do with the rest of her furniture filled her agenda that afternoon. Most had been sold earlier, but there were a few odds and end pieces she gave away. The cash would come in handy the next couple of weeks.

She'd sucked down caffeine in various forms all day. Hot, cold, it didn't matter. But no food.

As she cruised into Village Grove, a town larger than Dalton Springs, her stomach growled, and she was getting tired.

The golden arches loomed a couple of blocks ahead. Did she dare? Generally, the fast food place was the least expensive option.

A quick glance into the back seat and she knew her girls were still asleep. Katie, the oldest at nearly three, sat with her head cock-eyed and her neck crooked, her mouth agape and drooling. A thin shaft of fine baby-blonde hair was stuck to her face in her slobber. Fourteen-month-old Karly's right cheek was pressed hard up against the sidewall of her car seat, her one shock of blonde sticking straight up like a Mohawk. She clutched a beat-up Tickled-Pretty-Pink stuffed bear in her chubby little fingers.

Shelley looked back at the road, slowed, and pulled into the drive-through lane.

"Please let them sleep," she whispered, wanting a few minutes more of peace and quiet. Pulling slowly to the speaker, she rolled down her window.

A screech and a crackle met her. "Take your order?" the young man bellowed.

"Shit," she breathed and glanced back. Katie stirred. "A cheeseburger value meal," she said quietly, "and a large iced tea, please."

A scream went up from the back seat. Karly.

"Don! Don! Don!"

"Five-ninety-six, Ma'am. Please pull to the first window."

"Dammit," she hissed then smiled into the speaker. "Make that three of everything, please."

"Don! Don! Don!"

"Except the tea. Give me two juices instead."

"Yes, ma'am. Fifteen-seventy-two."

"Okay."

"Mom-meeee!" Katie shouted. "Karly woke me up! Oh! We're at 'Donald's! Can we play?"

"Slide! Slide!" Karly bounced in her seat.

"No, girls, we are not getting out."

Wails rose from the rear.

"Don! Don!"

Shelley sighed. "I have your food coming up. Hold on, girls."

She moved to the window and waited, pinching her nose while the girls chattered and bounced and squealed in the back seat. Karly still wanted to slide, and now Katie was yelling for her fries. In the end, she retrieved her meals from the window, pulled over and took the girls inside to eat. They did, barely, and then ran off to play in the huge play place while Shelley rubbed her temple and watched from a small table next to the multi-colored ball pit.

Luckily, the play place was nearly deserted. A quick glance outside told her why. Snow pelted down at a nice clip now. People must be staying in. Or they were out shopping.

She was getting a damn headache. Should get on the road soon, she kept thinking. Then she remembered she had to stop and get diapers before she got to Harbor Falls. Ralph's was at the end of town. She'd stop there.

One more stop. One more time getting the girls out, and back in, the car. Buckling, securing, tucking, finding bears, having snacks within reach, making sure straps weren't too tight. Another shopping trip trying to avoid the "mommy I wants" and the "gimmee gimmees" while searching for diapers, and oh, yes, she also needed wipes.

Can't forget the wipes.

All in all, she calculated that stopping at Ralph's, coupled with the hour they would probably spend here at 'Dons,' her arrival back in Harbor Falls would be later than anticipated. Of course, no one was expecting her, so what difference did it make, anyway?

She rubbed her head more. Too damn tired. She really, really needed to get going.

And going she did. She rounded up the little boogers, made her trek through Ralph's and was headed into Harbor Falls from the east side of town when she popped over the hill near the old Casey farm. The snow was coming in sideways now, and she was glad to almost be at Suzie's, even though her stomach was in a knot. She had no clue how her sister would react at her arrival.

She sighed. It had already been a long day and now...

Lights flashed in her rearview mirror and a siren chirped behind her. The girls started crying again. She glanced up.

"*Dammit!* Dammit all to hell."

Tears immediately sprung into her eyes. This, she did not need. *What next?*

Chapter Two

"This was a mistake."

Icy and sharp, the snow slanted against him as Matt got out of his cruiser and headed toward the blue Dodge. It cut into his face and he tilted his chin into his chest to avoid it. The driver moved the car to the side of the narrow road, but he wondered about the sanity of pulling it over. Visibility was quickly becoming non-existent and he didn't relish being exposed and vulnerable should someone else pop over that hill.

They'd had a lot of snow lately. An unusual amount. It didn't seem to be letting up any, either.

Before he'd left the cruiser, he'd taken a moment to jot down the license plate number, noting the out-of-county plates. He didn't recognize the car and figured the person inside wasn't local. Somehow that comforted him, although he wasn't quite sure why. Perhaps he would feel less guilty giving a ticket to a stranger rather than someone he knew—especially during the holidays.

He glanced at his watch. His day was nearly up. "Short and quick," he told himself. "Then get home."

The windows on the car were tinted so it was difficult to see inside. That always made him wary. He approached slowly, came even with the front edge of the side door, and knocked on the driver's window.

The immediate sound of babies crying hit him as the window rolled down. He leaned forward. A woman was turned toward the back seat. He stepped closer to see the driver. A blond mane was all he could see. She faced the children as her frantic voice tried to quiet them.

"Be still. Hush, girls," she said. He thought he heard a sniff behind that plea.

"Ma'am." He leaned further and looked at the passenger seat. No one there. He relaxed inside but kept his stoic composure from an outward appearance.

He hoped.

The woman turned to look at him and, in a flurry of words and tears, blurted out, "Officer, I'm so sorry. The babies were crying and I have a headache and," *sniff, sniff,* "the snow is coming and I wanted to get to my sister's and," *sniff,* "I didn't realize I was going that fast and—oh, my—"

She stopped. Blinked. Looked up at him with those baby blues that he remembered oh, so well. The baby blues that sometimes still haunted his sleep.

Something punched him deep. His gut twisted and fell. His heart slammed against his chest. Straightening his shoulders and posture, he attempted to plaster the most stoic demeanor he could possibly muster on his face.

He wasn't sure he pulled it off.

The snow angled into her window and the swiped at the tears spilling onto her cheeks. A hand shielded her eyes from the stinging pellets. "Matt?"

He nodded with a single word. "Shelley."

That's right. Show no emotion.

"I...uh..."

He squared himself. "Been a while since you were in town, so guess you don't know the speed limit has changed. Might be a good idea for you to heed that."

With a puzzled look, she nodded. "Of course."

"Of course," he echoed. "Since you left out of here on a whim and a prayer, without a word to anyone, I figured you've probably not given anyone in Harbor Falls a single thought since then, let alone the speed limit."

"Matt, I—"

He cut her off. "I'm giving you a warning. Watch it." With that, he turned on his heel and headed back to his cruiser, his heart pounding more with each step he took. *Yes, watch it sister. You have a lot of nerve showing your face back in this town.*

No, he wasn't going there.

By the time he settled himself in the cruiser, the breath whooshed out of him in one fell swoop, fogging up his windshield.

"Dammit," he muttered and kicked up the defroster.

He waited for her to ease back onto the road before pulling out himself, then he followed her all the way through town. He sat, back rigid, fingers curled in a tight grip around the steering wheel, his chest taut as a drum.

His brain hummed. His heart ached.

She turned onto Lake Road. Seemed she was heading toward Sweet Hart Inn. He headed up the mountain.

He couldn't wait to get home. To his cave.

"Dammit, Shelley, why are you here?" He pounded the dashboard.

Everyone in Harbor Falls knew that Cliff had died, but...

His gut slammed against his backbone. Was Shelley home? Was his high school sweetheart back in town to stay? The woman who sent him into his cave in the first place?

He hoped with everything in him that it wasn't true. It

was the holidays, right? Lots of people come home for the holidays. Even people who vanish from your life and never look back.

Hell, he hadn't realized how much his heart still hurt.

~

There were a million things she could feel right now, but Shelley pushed every one of them into some gray area of her brain. Matt was one. She could not deal with Matt Branson today. Not now.

The day had been too long. She was exhausted, emotional, and hungry again, not to mention frustrated with the crying babies in the back seat. Tired from fighting the snow and her emotions, she chose not to think any longer, just to do. So that is what she did.

She drove straight down Lake Road, turned into Suzie's drive, slanted her gaze at the sign that read, *Welcome to Sweet Hart Inn,* and prayed that she would be exactly that —welcomed.

She doubted it.

She knew the way even though she had never been to the house since Suzie had turned it into a bed and breakfast. Their Aunt Donna had lived there for all of Shelley's growing up years until she passed away—not long after she and Cliff had eloped and settled their lives into Dalton Springs. Shelley hadn't attended her aunt's funeral, either, and she felt a pang of guilt because of it. But things were as they were then, and there was nothing she could do about it now. What she *was* doing was what needed to be done—making amends, she hoped, with her sister and family—and that's all she could do.

Right now, at least. Any other past transgressions she'd deal with in time. Matt's face flashed into her mind's eye at that moment and just as quickly, she pushed the image away.

Not now.

The gray, snowy night matched her somber mood perfectly. The snow had stopped for a while. A couple of inches piled up around Suzie's front porch. She pulled alongside the house, and not bothering with anything but her purse and the girls, headed up the sidewalk. Karly was in her arms, her soft head resting on her shoulder. Katie toddled along beside her, holding her hand.

"Be careful of the ice, honey," she said to her oldest.

"Yes, Mommy."

Tears sprang to her eyes again at the sweet child. She loved her girls so much, and now that they had arrived at this decisive moment—as she navigated the steps up to Suzie's front porch with her most precious cargo—she wanted only one thing. She wanted Suzie to love her girls as much as she did.

Even if she didn't accept Shelley, maybe she'd accept her girls.

Too much to expect, probably.

With every emotion known to woman ready to cackle up and spill over inside of her, Shelley swallowed her pride and moved forward onto the porch. A cascade of greenery and lights arched over the front door. Beyond in the sidelights of the door, she could see someone milling about. Soft Christmas music met her ears and she could smell cookies baking.

Peanut butter with chocolate drops.

That notion made her smile. This was the Suzie she remembered.

If only...

The door swung abruptly open. "Shelley? Oh my God!"

Her sister stood there, framed by holly and twinkling lights, a questioning expression on her face. Her strawberry blond hair was piled high on her head. She had flour on her face and was wiping her hands on her apron. A little boy clung to her leg.

Tears poured. "Suzie," Shelley sobbed. "I'm so sorry. I am so, so sorry for everything. I am..."

Suzie grasped her sister and pulled her into the house, tears streaming down her face. "Come here, you," she whispered and kicked the door shut behind her. "Just come here."

Shelley sobbed on her sister's shoulder, and Suzie, always the gracious hostess, let her. She hugged her with several years' worth of longing, trapping the girls in their embrace.

"I've been so worried about you," Suzie whispered, pulling back to look into her face. She gently thumbed away tears from Shelley's eyes and then turned to both girls, cupping first Karly's small face in her hands, and leaning down to do the same with Katie. "You are both so beautiful," she said softly.

Next, she grasped the little boy's hand that still clutched her leg. Shelley guessed he was a little younger than Karly.

Crouching, she said to the boy. "Petey, these are your cousins, Katie and Karly. Say hello?"

Petey turned his face into his mother's leg. Katie burrowed a little closer into her own mother.

Straightening then, Suzie looked long into Shelley's face and whispered, "Merry Christmas, Shelley. We have a lot of catching up to do but let's put one thing to rest right now. The past is the past. And I am so very glad that you're here."

Shelley sobbed, relief washing over her.

Matt drove on autopilot up the mountain and past the old lodge, navigated the drifting snow on the narrow mountain road, and took his time getting to his isolated cabin. His escape. His refuge from the storm—and life.

Shelley was back, he was sure of it. As he'd thought over the situation of thirty minutes earlier, he realized that her car was packed up with things. A suitcase was jammed between the girl's two car seats. A couple of small boxes and bags were stowed in the passenger seat and floorboard. There was a grocery bag from Ralph's, too. He'd taken all of that in within a few seconds because that was what he was trained to do. Observe and record in his brain. Sometimes the details didn't jump back at him until he had removed himself from the situation and his brain had time to work over it.

The drive gave him more than enough time to analyze the situation.

He approached his cabin and pulled up close to the porch, realizing that he was going to have to shovel himself out in the morning. He wasn't going to worry about that now. Shoveling came with the territory when you lived at a higher elevation and winter was here. Besides, he welcomed the physical exertion. Although snowstorms in the Blue Ridge Mountains were a part of life here, rarely did they get one that shut their world down for long lengths of time. But they did get them occasionally, and when they did, residents in and around Harbor Falls generally were prepared to hole up for a few days.

He hoped that wasn't the case with this storm. Just like he hoped that Shelley would land in Harbor Falls for the holidays and then leave to go back to Dalton Springs. That scenario was not likely, and he knew it.

Fiddling with the door lock, he twisted the knob and stepped inside. He shrugged out of his jacket and shoes, handing up the coat on a hook by the door and leaving his shows on a mat there as well. Glancing toward the fireplace, he decided to light a fire to take the chill off. The furnace was set to a low temperature while he was gone, but a fire was what he wanted and needed tonight.

A fire would chase the chill away from his bones and his heart. Hell, he hated that his heart had turned cold after all these years, but it had. There was a time he thought if he ever had the chance to win Shelley back, he would do it. But that time had long passed.

How many years was a man supposed to wait?

Chapter Three

P etey and Karly hit it off immediately. In no time, they were toddling about, circling the Christmas tree in the living room, and playing hide and seek in every nook and cranny downstairs. Katie poked at a homemade chicken potpie that Suzie had popped out of the freezer and baked for her.

"I'm sorry she's such a picky eater," Shelley said, sitting at the bar and scooping cookies off the sheet to cool on racks. "Always has been."

Katie looked up and smiled at her mother. "I picky."

Shelley grinned. "Yes, unfortunately, and you know it."

Suzie worked the cornbread stuffing with her hands, mixing up the ingredients. "No problem. Petey is as picky as they come too. Some days all he will eat are my chicken potpies and sweet pickles. Breakfast, lunch and dinner. That's why I keep them on hand."

"Good idea. I need to learn how to cook like you."

Suzie smiled. "You've been busy with babies. That will come later, if you want."

Shelley thought about that and smiled. What would her

future bring? "I just don't know what I want to do with my life."

"That will come too." Reaching out, Suzie patted her hand. "Have you called Mama and Daddy yet?"

She shook her head. "No. I need a few more minutes." Suzie nodded and Shelley was relieved her sister didn't push it.

They talked for over an hour while Suzie managed to feed everyone and simultaneously do prep work for the meals she was catering tomorrow, on Christmas Eve. Brad was at the lodge for the employee Christmas party, and Suzie didn't expect him until late. That was nice because it gave them time to themselves. They'd discussed Suzie's marriage, the renovation of the lodge, the births of all the babies, and even Cliff's death.

"That had to be horrible," Suzie said, as they chatted about the shock of the accident. "I didn't realize cement mixers could do so much damage to a Honda."

"Anything running over you full-speed-ahead is going to be bad."

"At least he didn't know what hit him."

"True," Shelley replied, her gaze drifting. "If only he hadn't taken that detour and swerved for that dog."

"Freak accident."

"Yeah." *Pause.* Shelley pondered the freakishness of it all.

"Cliff always liked dogs," Suzie added.

"Yeah. It was a Bassett Hound."

Pause.

"How do you know?" Suzie picked at a piece of lint on a dishcloth.

"The truck driver said it in his statement. Said the dog lumbered off okay but poor Cliff got smashed like a people pancake." Shelley sighed. "Funny how people remember details like that."

Suzie giggled a little. "Sorry. It's just..."

Shelley grinned. "I know. It's okay. It is funny in an odd way."

"Makes sense though."

"What?"

"That he wouldn't want to hit the dog. Not the people pancake part."

Shelley nodded. "Oh. Sure." She was surprised and a little appalled at herself that she could even think this way about poor Cliff. Maybe humor was a way to deal.

A longer pause. Suzie looked straight into her eyes. "Shelley, you know we wanted to help you."

The mood shifted then, and she waited a moment to respond. "I know. I couldn't."

"You could have returned our calls. Mama and Daddy were so troubled."

That cut deeper than she anticipated. "I figured."

Suzie looked up from her mixing bowl. "Shelley, why? Why would you not let us help you through this? I know we were sort of joking around there a few minutes ago but this was a serious thing for you. Losing a husband is an awful, terrible thing. And it was so sudden." She bit her lip and stared ahead. "Besides, Cliff was, well...family. Sort of."

She'd thought her eyes were pretty much devoid of tears but at that, they stung again. "I assumed you all hated me."

Sighing, Suzie went to the sink and rinsed her hands, then stood at the bar and placed her palms on it. "Shelley, don't ever think anything stupid like that again."

She shrugged and stood. "Suzie! I stole your man! You went out of town to work at that job, so you could save money to open your own business, and I swooped in and stole him. He was lonely, and I was young and flirty, and before I knew it, we were in bed and I had fallen in love with him. Why would you not hate me?"

Suzie laughed. "Oh, believe me, I did." She moved around

the bar, tugged out a stool, and sat. She pulled Shelley into a seat, too. "I hated you with a passion, but not because you stole Cliff. I hated you because you had something I wanted. A loving husband and a family. But all of that changed once Brad and Petey came into my life. Over the months, I realized I didn't hate you after all. In fact, you cleared the way for me to pursue the happiness I always wanted. Happiness that Cliff couldn't give me." She paused for a moment. "I can't imagine what it is like to lose a husband. Now that I have Brad..." she trailed off, thinking, "well, I felt for you, and wanted to help in some way, but you didn't respond. I didn't know what to do."

Shelley shook her head. "There was nothing you could do. I had to find my way out of this." She glanced off, and then added. "But Suzie, I can't do it. I wasn't making it in Dalton Springs on my own. I lost my house. The money wouldn't stretch. So, I needed..."

"You need to start over. Here. In Harbor Falls." Suzie reached for Shelley's hands. "You're home now, sweetie, and this time, you'd better let us help you."

Hesitant, Shelley grasped back. "I do need your help," she whispered. "Just for a while. I swear, once I get back on my feet I'll be fine, and I'll never be a burden to you again."

Suzie shook her head. "You're not a burden now."

"I hope not."

Suzie squeezed her hands. "You're not. We'll work out the details later. When Brad gets home, I'll have him fetch your things from your car and get you settled in upstairs. For now, it's Christmas and we are going to have the best one in years. Now, go call Mama and tell her you are here, or I will. I can't wait for tomorrow night."

Shelley couldn't either. It would be the first Christmas she would have with her family in years. Her Mama and Daddy had never even seen her girls.

A smile broke across Suzie's face, but Shelley also noticed

her misty eyes. Suzie was on the verge of tears. "I can't either, Suzie. Thank you for everything. I'll go call them now."

~

L ater, as Shelley lay in bed in Suzie's guest room, she thought about the numerous twists of fate life had dealt her. She refused to feel lonely and depressed any longer about all that, now that she was here. Now that she was home.

The hard part was history. She was going to make this work.

Shelley was tired but happy—and settling into this beautiful room provided her the comfort she needed right now. Suzie had called this the blue room, but really, it was mostly white with blue accents. All the furniture was white—the picture frames, the billowy sheers at the window and the plantation blinds underneath—all set against a backdrop of watercolor blue walls. The Irish quilt was navy and white, the sheets pale cobalt with starched cotton embroidered pillowcases, and a matching crocheted afghan tossed over an old over-stuffed chair. Blue Willow plates were on the wall and a blue-swirled glass ball hung from the curtain rod. The room had a beachy feel, which was a nice contrast in this mountain area.

The girls were asleep in the adjoining room—the turquoise room. Suzie always names her bedrooms after colors. Lucky for everyone, Suzie didn't take guests over the holidays. That meant she only had to share her bathroom with the girls, which was normal for them. Situated between the two rooms, it was also provided easy access to them. She could hear their cries and whimpers in the night.

So tired she could barely spit, she laid wide-awake looking up at the ceiling. Seemed it was difficult to turn off her brain and calm down her body. The worse part was over, though, apologizing to Suzie. Tomorrow she'd see her parents again, and she couldn't wait for them to see her girls. Her mother cried on the phone and wanted to rush right over, but Shelley convinced her that they were all tired and tomorrow would be better. Her dad finally talked some sense into her.

Her mama's last words on the phone had both pained and relieved her.

"I'll sleep better tonight than I have in years."

Nearly choking, Shelley quickly said her goodbye and hung up.

This was a beginning. A fresh start. She still had a long road ahead of her.

Turning onto her side, she closed her eyes. Just at the point of giving over to sleep, an image popped into her head.

An unsettling but nice image. Tall, broad shoulders, sandy-brown hair, eyes the color of a copper penny, and in uniform.

Matt.

Something clutched at her heart. He looked good. Damn good. No doubt, some young chic had snatched him up in no time with minutes to spare. She hoped so. He deserved someone. Someone who would be good to him.

She supposed she'd find out, eventually.

It was good seeing him though. He was her first love. Her first...everything.

Since you left out of here on a whim and a prayer, without a word to anyone, I figured you've probably not given Harbor Falls another thought.

He was wrong. She had thought of Harbor Falls, and of him, often.

But she'd dumped him. Obviously, he'd not forgotten about that. Odd how that notion bothered her.

Chapter Four

"*H*old onto you hats, folks, we're in for a heckuva snowstorm. What we saw yesterday was nothing compared to what's coming. This new front started rolling across Missouri and western Tennessee the past twenty-four hours, and the computers tell us it could be a doozey. So get those gifts wrapped and delivered and batten down the hatches. Santa, you may be in for a cold, snowy ride tonight. I hate to say the B word, but...*"

Matt smashed his hand down on the clock radio beside his bed, halting the weatherman's prediction.

"Great..." he mumbled. "Blizzard."

He dozed again and five minutes later, *White Christmas* blared in his ear.

Smash!

The old clock radio slid off the oak bedside table. He glanced at it. Five minutes after six. Shit. Bing Crosby still crooned from the floor and then the DJ was back. "*Looks like we have a few hours, folks. Expect light snow to arrive around noon. We'll see six inches by dinnertime, and another two-to-three throughout the evening hours. Hey, we're not used to this folks, but look at the bright side—we'll have a good ol' fashioned white Christmas this year. Get those sleds ready, kids!"*

Groaning, Matt reached for the radio's cord and jerked it from the wall.

"Wonderful." Sitting up, he rubbed his hands over his face. He usually didn't work on Saturday but had taken a short shift for this morning. With this weather though, he predicted he'd probably get the call to work later, if needed.

Christmas Eve and a blizzard. Damn. With both of his sisters driving down from Ohio, his mother would be worried-to-a-fritter until they arrived. Not to mention he would likely spend his evening helping people—who should know better than to drive on winding mountain roads during a blizzard—get out of the ditch they'd slid into.

"Bah humbug."

It's all right. He would find time with family and besides, he was here to serve, protect, and help his community. It was his job—it was who he was.

Rising, he stumbled to the shower, wondering why he was in such a foul mood. Ah, yes, Shelley, combined with the effect of too much bourbon last night. So why the hell was he even up?

Oh, yeah. He'd volunteered for the early shift so he could go Christmas shopping later for his nieces and nephews. Nothing like waiting until the last minute but he was a procrastinator when it came to shopping, and he had to have gifts. Today.

Hot water rained down on his back and he reached up to switch the nozzle on the showerhead to deliver a harsher stream on his neck and shoulders.

"Oh. Yes..." he hissed.

Eyes closed, he tried to erase the vision of Shelley looking up at him with those movie-princess eyes, summer sky blue, and all that blond hair framing her face.

Tears.

Even stressed and upset, she was still beautiful.

"Dammit."

Worse part, she was clearly upset, and he had wanted to take her in his arms and smooth all the bad stuff away, whatever it was. Even after all this time, he'd been tempted, for a moment, to say, "How can I help? What can I do?" But he hadn't. Thank God. One touch to her face, one hint of her scent, one innocent and casual embrace could be his undoing.

No. He'd rescued many a damsel in distress in his day—was part of the job sometimes—but dammit if he'd risk rescuing her in any way shape or form. Shelley Hart was one woman who probably wouldn't welcome his rescuing her anyway. But he'd heard over the past few months that things weren't good for her and that did concern him. Still, he didn't want to get all White Knight and everything about her and think he could make her world right again.

That wouldn't happen.

Shelley made her choices long ago when she'd dumped him and ran straight into the arms of someone else.

Breathing deep, he let the water beat on his head and shoulders some more, hoping it would beat some sense into his thick skull at the same time. Then he stepped out the shower, dried off and dressed, and left the cabin to do whatever it was he needed to do today.

Work. And oh yeah, shopping. Right.

~

"I can't believe I forgot the baby wipes."

Slamming the door to her Dodge, Shelley muttered to herself and headed toward Ralph's. Only a ten-minute drive from Suzie's, the store parking lot looked fairly empty, and she hoped to sneak in and out with her purchase in record time.

Since it was still early, she figured most people would be home in bed. Wrapping her jacket tight around her against the stiff breeze, she flipped up her furry hood and hustled toward the entrance. With any luck, she'd see no one who would recognize her and want to talk.

She didn't need that this morning. Once she realized she'd forgotten the wipes, and that the babies would be up soon, she rushed out of the house without washing her face or brushing her teeth. Bad choice, likely, but she did it. Even though she pulled on a pair of jeans, she still wore the t-shirt she'd slept in. No bra.

Not the way to introduce herself back into Harbor Falls, by any means.

"Okay," she mumbled, her breath steaming from her lips, "shop like a man. Get in, get out, get home." The automatic door to Ralph's swished open and she moved inside.

"Yes," she hissed. "Practically empty."

Some weird rendition of *Jingle Bells* played in the background.

She scurried along to the baby aisle. Glancing right and left, she let her hood slip down to her shoulders and scoped the aisle for her brand. There. Yes. She grabbed it, tucked it under one arm, and rounded the corner. She was outta here.

Then—

Coffee.

The heavenly smell of coffee hit her full force. Oh, could she use some caffeine. Definitely. The dark kind with extra octane. Looking to her left, she spied the self-serve counter and smiled. Ralph's was moving up. She didn't remember this coffee service before.

Hesitant for only a second, she looked about. Oh my God, was that Betty Jo still checking at the counter? How many years had she worked for Ralph? A hundred? Another glance back to the coffee. Yes, she would risk it.

Darting forward, she realized she may actually be salivating, longing for the taste of the warm and rich liquid on her tongue. "I swear I must be addicted," she muttered as she reached for the largest of the paper cups.

"Okay, so where is the yellow stuff?" She searched for the artificial sweeteners, quickly located them, tore off the tops of three packets and dumped the contents into her empty cup. Next, she poured the coffee on top, the aroma wafting toward her nostrils.

"Um." She closed her eyes, inhaled, and savored a moment of pleasure. "Come to mama…"

"Ahem. You going to stand there and breathe that, or drink it?"

Her eyes popped open. Shelley jerked. *Shit!* "Matt?"

"Yes. Mind scooting over so I can get some of that, too?"

Shelley looked where she was standing, right in front of the burners and the carafe. "Oh. Oh!" She backed up and searched for the lids. She rounded him and they switched places. In the process, she scooted her hood up a little higher to cover her face.

"I need a lid," she said, then edged away. "Ouch. And one of those cardboard protector thingies…" She fumbled with the plastic disk and couldn't get it on straight to save her.

"Here, let me."

Large hands reached in front of her. She tried not to look at him. After all, she was skuzzy. Hadn't washed her face…

She ran her tongue over her teeth.

He deftly attached the lid, slipped a cardboard sleeve on the cup, and handed it to her. "There you go. Complete with one of those cardboard protector thingies."

Shelley looked up into his face. He almost grinned. "Thanks," she said.

"You're welcome."

He didn't move. Just stood there. She stared at her cup. "Well, I should be going."

"Me, too."

Finally, she did look up. He'd not gone anywhere. *Move or say something, Shelley!*

"After you," he said.

She took a step toward the cashier, then halted. "Oh, Matt. Thanks for last night. I mean, you could have given me a ticket." She swallowed and looked into his eyes, *really* looked into them, the first time in a long, long time. She had always thought his eyes were the most beautiful color of coppery brown...

He hesitated, looking like he wanted to say something, but couldn't find the right words. "You weren't going that much over the speed limit," he finally said.

She shrugged and held her coffee cup in both hands, clamping her left arm tight against the wipes still tucked into her left side. "Well, it was nice of you." She glanced at Betty Jo who was staring at them. "I should go."

She turned, slightly.

"At least one of us plays nice."

The tone of those words, as much as their implication, cut as deep as anything. She turned back. "Matt that was a long time ago."

"Three years, six months, seven days."

Shit. He hadn't... Had he? "What?"

"Three years, six months, seven days."

"Are you still mad at me?"

He squared himself, stance broad, as if ready for action. The look on his face said he meant business. "I'm mad as hell, Shelley. Why wouldn't I be?"

She had no clue. "I..." she glanced off. "I don't know what to say."

"Sorry, I think, is the appropriate word."

Looking at him again, she shook her head. "Somehow I think my saying sorry still won't cut it." She sat her coffee and the wipes down on the counter and reached for his forearm. "Matt..."

"It's a start." He jerked away, stepped back.

Surprised, she continued, "Matt, okay, I'm sorry. I know I hurt you. I hurt a lot of people and I'm sorry about all of that. I know..."

"You *know*? You don't know shit." He sat his coffee on the counter beside hers, although a little too hard. The bottom busted off the cup and hot coffee splattered everywhere. Both jumped, but he continued. "Hurt? Do you know the meaning of that word, Shelley? You made me the laughingstock of this entire damn town." His gaze narrowed and he leaned forward. "I don't ever, ever, want to see you again. Do you understand? So, if you are back in town for good, steer clear of me, you got that?"

Stunned, Shelley jerked back and stared into his face. "Sure. Got it. Perfectly clear."

Then he stomped off, leaving her standing there watching him walk away. She stood there until he left the store.

She guessed she just got from Matt what she had expected from her family. But could she blame him? She'd evidently hurt him bad—and obviously, he'd not gotten over it.

"Damn it."

She didn't move until Betty Jo came up with a mop.

"Shelley, dear, let me get this."

She stepped back and investigated Betty's facial expression. "Oh. Excuse me. I'm sorry Betty Jo. I didn't realize..."

No. She hadn't realized. No really. She'd been immersed in her own world and the concerns of others were second place. Truly, all this time, she had not known that Matt Branson hurt that badly when she broke it off with him—and ran off with Cliff.

"Takes time to heal," Betty Jo said, not looking up from her mopping.

"It was years ago."

"Yes," Betty answered, swiping the mop back and forth, "but small towns don't forget. Men don't forget. It's their ego."

Tears welled up in Shelley's eyes. "I guess not," she whispered.

Still looking at the door Matt had exited, she wondered if she would ever live down the actions of her past with the residents of this town. Especially, with Matt.

Somehow, it mattered. Now, it mattered.

"He's just hurt is all," Betty said.

Shelley finally looked at her. "I didn't know."

"You do now."

"He hates me."

Betty stopped her mopping and shook her head. "No, I don't think that's it, sweetie."

"But he said..."

"Men say a lot of things when they've been hurt bad." She patted her arm. "He'll come around."

Shelley wasn't so certain. "I don't know." Glancing at their feet, she noticed Betty Jo had everything cleaned up. "I'm sorry about this mess. Let me help." She grabbed some paper towels. "And then I'll pay for his coffee and stuff."

"Never mind about that." Betty took the towels out of her hands and picked up the baby wipes. "Let's check you out and get you back to the Inn. Two little girls I understand. I bet they are adorable."

Desperately trying to fight back tears, Shelley smiled and nodded, thankful for her kindness and change of subject. "Yes, and they are beautiful."

Betty Jo smiled. "Of course, they are!" She hooked her arm in Shelley's and led her toward the checkout counter.

"I need to get back before they wake up."

"Sure, honey." Betty Jo rounded the counter and scanned her purchases.

Wake up. Yeah. She supposed perhaps she was the one who needed the wakeup call this morning. Last night with Suzie had gone so well, she had hoped the rest of her reunion with Harbor Falls would be smooth sailing.

Apparently, that was not the case.

Families forgive. Old boyfriends do not.

Try as she might, the thought of that made her tears spill over. What was she going to do? No one in this town was going to let her forget the past. How could she move forward with the constant reminders all around her?

~

Matt sat in his cruiser in the parking lot at Ralph's and let out a long and painful explosion of breath. His chest felt like it was going to detonate from pent-up anger and yes, hurt. He hadn't meant to unleash on Shelley like that but the sight of her had caught him totally off guard. He'd only wanted coffee, not an encounter with the one woman he was not yet ready to encounter. Again.

Two times in less than twenty-four hours. *Don't make this a habit, Branson.*

He still needed coffee.

Obviously, if Shelley was going to frequent Ralph's for morning coffee, he needed to change his habit. Drumming his fingers on the steering wheel, he stared at the front door of the grocery and within seconds, Shelley emerged. He watched her slowly make her way to the older model Dodge Stratus he'd pulled over last night, swipe at her face and get in the car, and then drive off toward Maple Street. Was she crying? That thought bothered him a little. He hadn't meant to make her cry. He followed the path of her vehicle until her brake lights came on at the courthouse square. She turned left. From there, she had a straight shot down Elm toward Lake Road, which would take her to Suzie's.

He assumed that was where she was heading. He stared down the road long after her brake lights were gone.

At any rate, he'd change his morning routine. After twisting the key to start the cruiser, he followed Shelley's path but made a turn off Elm onto North Main, then he parked in front of *Sugar High Bakery*, wondering if that was a bad idea too.

Shelley's cousin, Sydney, owned the *Sugar High*. Was this borrowing trouble too?

But she had coffee. And he needed coffee. Now.

Sucking in a deep breath, he exited his vehicle, crossed the sidewalk, and entered the bakery. The aroma of fresh baked goods and coffee overtook him. Good choice.

"Matt!"

He glanced to his right. Over by the window sat his colleague and fellow Harbor Falls police officer Chris Marks. Matt gave Chris a nod then glanced to the counter as he headed toward the table. Sydney caught his eye and said, "Black, right?"

"Yes, ma'am. And something sweet if you don't mind."

"That's the way we do it around here, sugar." Sydney winked and Matt smiled. "Good to see you out and about." Shelley's cousin had always been the friendly type and a straight shooter. There would be no games played here, he was certain. He wondered if Sydney knew Shelley was back in town.

Not his business to bring it up and he wouldn't.

He sat across from Chris. "Morning. What's up?"

Chris sat staring out the window. "Not a lot. Slow morning. I got patrol out on the east end in thirty minutes. Thought I'd stop in here for a few first."

Matt dipped his head in a quick nod. Sydney placed a steaming cup of black coffee in front of him and a gigantic glazed donut. "Here you go, Matt. Fresh out of the fryer. The glaze hasn't even hardened yet. Did you know Shelley was back in town?"

So, there it was. He glanced up into Sydney's face. "I did. And we're not going to talk about that."

Sydney screwed up her mouth. "I heard about it last night. Shelley's mom called my mom, and my mom called me. You know it was only a matter of time until she realized she needed family and all. And those two little girls, they need family too. I can't wait to see them. We are all going over there tonight."

Matt took a deep breath and exhaled. Sydney's sentences always seemed to flow together, and he wasn't sure how or if she took a breath while she was speaking—so he took a breath for her. "That's nice to hear. I hope you have a good time." He looked at Chris then, who was still staring out the window. Intent on changing the subject, he said, "What's got your attention, Marks?"

But Sydney went on. "Oh, that's Katie Long. The librarian. Chris sits here every morning watching her walk from the parking lot into the library wearing those tight, short skirts of hers and those three-inch stiletto heels."

Chris' brow furrowed as he turned to Sydney. "I do not."

"It's why you come here," Sydney countered.

"I come here for the coffee," said Chris.

Sydney placed both of her palms on the table and leaned forward. "As much as I would love to believe that, Chris Marks, I say bull hockey. You come here for the legs."

Matt grinned and watched Chris's face turn crimson. He glanced across the street. "Good looking librarian, huh? I haven't been to the library lately."

Chris frowned. "Well don't start now."

That's the last thing Matt needed, and he knew it. "Relax, Marks. I have no desire to tangle with the librarian. She's all yours to ogle."

"I'm not ogling."

Sydney stood and sighed. "Oh God, Chris. You are so ogling."

Matt laughed as Chris sputtered. "I... I..."

Then she turned to Matt. "Might do you a little good to ogle too, once in a while, Matt Branson. You're gonna dry up and get old before you know it and your life is going to pass you by."

Now it was Matt's turn to frown. "What the hell are you talking about?"

She leaned in again. "She's back. Make your move, Matt, before someone else in this town does. You'll kick your own ass from here to Asheville and back if you don't, and if she goes off and marries someone else again. Because you know it's going to happen eventually."

Matt swallowed and narrowed his gaze. "Don't go there, Sydney. I'm not ready."

"You better get ready."

He shook his head. "You don't understand."

Sydney shifted her weight to her left hip. "I understand perfectly. It was bad. Real bad. For a lot of us, but really bad for you and you've not gotten over it. Over her. But she's back. Make no mistake, she's vulnerable, and you don't need to rush in there like a house afire, but don't push her away before you and she even have a chance."

Matt stood and looked Sydney square in the eyes. "Stay out of this, Sydney."

"She's my cousin. And you are my friend. I'm in it."

"I'm asking you to stay out."

"All I'm saying, Matt, is that you might want to be a little nicer to her than you were this morning. She's had a rough time too."

This morning? "What the hell are you taking about, Syd?"

She shrugged. "News travels fast. Small town, you know? She was crying when she left Ralph's and feels like no one here is ever gonna give her a break again."

Shit. "Well people need to be cautious."

Sydney eyed him. "Sometimes people just need to throw caution to the wind, Matt Branson. Sometimes people just need to take their heart and run with it."

Chapter Five

"I was hoping you could help me out today, Shelley, if you don't mind. I know it's Christmas Eve, but, I could really use an extra pair of hands."

Suzie dumped a pan of piping hot potatoes into a huge colander in the sink. Steam rose and she turned her head to look at her sister. "The pies and cakes are on the shelves in the pantry, in boxes and ready to go. I have the name and order number on each. You'll see a little sticker on the top. The salads are in the fridge in the basement. We'll have to carry those up at the last minute. Same deal, sticker on top. The hot foods will be coming out in the next couple of hours. I have to do some shifty work here." She glanced up at the clock. "Great. It's just after noon now. Everything must be delivered by six and we're racing the snow. Oh, the list is on the bulletin board."

She pointed toward the wall above the built-in kitchen desk. "Matter of fact, could you go check that now and see what time we need to be at Clint Roberts' house? He called earlier this week and wanted to know if his delivery could be moved up. Poor man, eating alone on Christmas day." She peered at her sister. "And such a fine specimen. He really shouldn't be eating alone. Perhaps we should invite him over."

Shelley narrowed her gaze. "Clint Roberts? Stop. I know that look."

"What look?"

"That, *let's fix her up* look." Suzie had loved to try to find dates for her little sister all during high school. "I'm not ready, Suzie."

Suzie grimaced. "Oh, hell. Last thing on my mind."

Moving toward the list, Shelley looked for Clint's name. "Four o'clock."

Suzie hefted the colander of potatoes onto the counter and dumped them in a huge mixing bowl. "What?" She batted away steam again.

"Clint. He wants his meal delivered at four."

"Oh." Two huge sticks of butter went into the potatoes. "Wouldn't hurt for you to put yourself back out there though."

Frowning, Shelley replied, "Um, No. Maybe in another year or so." Suddenly she felt flushed, thinking about her encounter with Matt earlier this morning. With her reputation, there wasn't man in Harbor Falls who would touch her with a ten-foot pole.

"Well, Clint's not right for you anyway."

"Not sure anyone is right for me," she mumbled.

Suzie thoroughly salted and peppered the potatoes. "What about Matt?"

Shelley coughed. "Yeah right."

"Well, you two were very much in love in high school, and he's still holding a torch for you, I think."

She laughed aloud at that one. "Oh, I don't think so."

Reaching for the cream, Suzie stopped to look at her sister. "Why would you say that?"

She hesitated, and then decided to spill. "I've already seen

Matt. Twice, in fact. He pulled me over for speeding last night on the way into town, but he let me off with a warning. Then, I ran into him again at Ralph's this morning when I went in to get the wipes. Believe me, he's not interested. In fact, he was darned blunt. I think his words were something like, 'if you are back to stay, steer clear of me.' Doesn't sound like torch-holding to me."

"Sounds exactly like it to me."

Vigorously, Shelley shook her head. "No. Believe me. He's not interested. He's mad as hell. So, I'll do as he said and leave him alone." She looked sharply at her sister. "And you will too! Do you hear me?"

Suzie turned to pour a cup of cream into the potatoes. "Of course. Whatever you say, sis."

After a pause, Suzie added. "But he looks good, doesn't he? Filled out in the past couple of years. Works out a lot, I think. And in the uniform..."

Shelley closed her eyes and immediately got a mental image. "Yes, dammit, he looks good." *Too good.* She shook herself and opened her eyes. "But that is neither here nor there. Matt Branson is no longer a part of my life, and he made it perfectly clear that he wants nothing to do with me. So, don't go getting any ideas."

Suzie turned toward her sister and grinned. "Noted. Now, who is on that list before Clint? This snow is coming down and we might need to move everyone up. Will you check?"

∽

S*ometimes people just need to take their heart and run with it.*

Matt knew what Sydney meant and he knew that for years he had been doing just the opposite. Oh, he'd been running all right—running away from his hurt, avoiding the subject of

Shelley every chance he got, pushing away from a close relationship with any woman. But with all of that running, he'd left his heart out of it every single, damn time. Easier that way, he knew.

He didn't intend to risk the pain again.

He'd become a master at protecting his heart, not running with it. In fact, the thought of throwing caution to the wind and going after Shelley just about made him nauseous. He'd not brought his heart out to play since the day she told him they were done—and he had no intention of bringing it out any time soon—with her or with any other woman.

He sighed, watching snowflakes drift over his windshield as he sat in the same place he sat last night when he'd pulled Shelley over. Thank God, his shift was over at noon today. He had things to do before the Christmas Eve family events tonight. He was ready to get those tasks done because the longer he sat there, the more he thought about Shelley. He had to admit, that the few minutes he had stood looking down at her last night had been a huge jolt to his heart. His ego. And messed with his head a little.

She was beautiful, even while crying. He'd always thought she was pretty and sexy, even when they were teenagers. It didn't matter if she was scuffed up and dirty playing softball in a field, or if she were dressed to the nines in a little black dress with pearls. He'd always liked her looks and any time he ever saw her, his heart lit up.

But it was more than the fact that she was a pretty girl. His heart just felt happy whenever she was around. He was happy.

Caught off guard last night, it had happened then too. His heart, for the first time in years, lit up at the sight of her. Her dewy eyes tugged at his heartstrings. Her lips were still pink and kissable, and how he had remembered kissing those lips for minutes on end when they were younger....

His heart hurt, dammit. His chest was tight. He hadn't felt

anything in that spot for months. Nothing. Because he hadn't *let* his heart feel. He'd shut off the pain and yes, even the good feelings.

Dammit, Shelley! Don't do this to me. Don't make me feel.

But he *could* feel now, and the pain was real. He ached for her today just like he'd ached for her the day she'd left. He remembered how that felt like it was yesterday. She'd given him no real reason why she wanted to break up—just that she wanted to move on, and she felt like he should too. That they had grown up since high school and they had different goals. She'd never mentioned anyone else or wanting to be with anyone else.

It didn't make sense.

A week later it all came together. The news flew all over town like an out-of-control wildfire. Shelley Hart had run off and married her sister's fiancé—one week after he and Shelley had broken up.

It damned near killed him.

And Sydney wondered why he was cautious?

Shelley crossed her arms and leaned into the desk, searching the delivery list. "You want me to be the delivery girl?"

Nodding, Suzie pushed back a stray lock of hair with her forearm. Shelley went to her and clipped it back into place. "Thank you. That hair was bugging the tar out of me." She paused, reaching for the potato masher.

Shelley went on. "If you don't mind that the girls are here with you, I can deliver, run errands, whatever you need."

A huge sigh of relief escaped Suzie's lips. She tweaked her sister's cheek. "Thank God you came home. I can use some help. I'll let Brad deal with the kids."

About that time a squeal, a giggle, and a man's low chuckle came from the living room.

Suzie grinned. "I just love that." Then immediately, she frowned and reached for Shelley's hand. "Sorry, I didn't mean..."

Shelley stopped her. "It's fine. Really. I'm glad you have Brad. And the girls sure love him already. He's read them at least three stories this morning."

"He's really good with kids."

"They miss their dad." She glanced off.

Suzie went to her then and gave Shelley a hug. "Of course, they do honey. They will be adjusting to life without him for a long time. So will you."

"I know. Being here is helping though, Suzie. Thank you."

Suzie gave her another squeeze. Shelley pulled back, nodding toward the cackle of laughter from the living room. "They were calling him Uncle Bad a minute ago."

Laughing, Suzie went back to work on the hot spuds. "That fits." She looked at Shelley with a twinkle. "He is a bad, bad boy..."

"Suzie!"

"Well, it's true. And I love it." She mashed some more, slowed, paused, and looked back up at Shelley.

"What?" She wasn't sure she liked that look on her face.

"Shelley, I have more work than I can handle."

The buzzer went off on the oven. Shelley trotted over to turn it off then looked inside. "I think the cornbread stuffing is finished.

"Test it for me, huh?"

Glancing around, Shelley picked up a thin-blade knife and stuck it in the middle. Came out clean. Then she pushed the stuffing away from the side of the pan. Yes. It was done. "Ready here," she told her sister.

"Hm. Good."

Grabbing potholders, Shelley pulled the steaming pan of stuffing out of the oven and set it on a wooden cutting board on the counter. Once more, she pressed a finger into the dish to see if it would bounce back. Yes.

"It's done."

"Good."

"Shelley?"

"Hm?"

"I need help."

She turned to her sister. "I know. I'll do your deliveries today."

"No. No, that's not what I mean." She sat the masher down on the counter and faced her sister. "I know you don't want handouts, and this is definitely not a handout. I've had more work in the past six months than I did in the first two years of my business. The inn is going strong. The second cookbook is in the can. It comes out in two months and the publisher wants me to do a book tour. I've nearly stopped doing my cooking classes because of the time factor, although I dearly love to do them. And the catering, sweet Jesus, the catering is my bread and butter right now since the inn is closed until February. I need your help."

Stunned, Shelley took a step back. "You want me to work for you?"

Suzie shook her head. "No, with me. Be my partner. You always loved to cook, and you're a natural. I can teach you the rest. With Petey now, and with Brad so busy at the lodge on top of everything else, I need you. Big time."

Shelley sat on a barstool. "I don't know what to say."

Suzie grinned. "Say yes. Please."

"Yes?"

"Well, that was enthusiastic."

"Yes!"

"Ack!" Suzie jumped up and down. Shelley sprung up too

and they hugged, squealing. Suzie stopped and grasped her forearms. "Seriously, I don't think you will want for work. Sydney could also use some help in the bakery part-time. I told her I would mention it to you."

"Seriously?"

"Yep."

Some sort of seriously elated happy energy bubbled up inside Shelley. "That's fabulous!"

The pitter-patter of stockinged feet and little girl giggles joined them. "Mama!" Katie shrieked. "Uncle Bad got my toes!"

Shelley scooped her up. "Well, did he give them back? Let me see!" She grasped for one of Katie's feet.

A silly smile broke across the girl's face. "Bad didn't really take 'em. They still on my feets."

"What's all this?" Brad's voice boomed out.

Suzie grinned from ear to ear. "She said yes."

"Thank God." He reached for his wife and nuzzled her ear. "Maybe I can get my Suzie back at least part-time for a while." He kissed her cheek. "Did you tell her about the lodge?"

Shelley looked from Brad to Suzie. "What? What about the lodge?"

Suzie nudged him. "You tell her."

"All right." He looked into Shelley's eyes and even though she'd only met him the night before, she knew he was a sincere man and anticipated what he was about to say. She could see some seriousness in his thought. "The top floor of the lodge has a three-bedroom suite with two bathrooms. It is yours for as long as you need it. Rent free."

The breath whooshed out of her the second her butt hit the barstool. Her hands fluttered to her chest, stilling her heart. "Oh, no. Brad, I couldn't."

Brad leaned closer and placed his hands on her shoulders.

"Yes, you can. We want you there with the girls. There's no kitchen, but you can use the hotel kitchen anytime you like. I know the head chef." He winked and stepped back. "Besides, when I cook, I cook plenty, and there will always be enough for you and the girls. Raid the refrigerator."

Almost giddy with excitement, Shelley was speechless. "I... Brad, Suzie, I don't know... this is too much. I don't think I can accept."

Suzie crossed her arms over her chest. "Hey, little sister. It's Christmas. Think of it as your gift. You gonna refuse your Christmas present?"

Again, Shelley glanced from her sister to Brad. "I, uh... I don't know what to say..."

"Say yes," they chimed simultaneously.

"All right. Yes! But this is only temporary until I can get my own place. I want you to know that I realize that." Her gaze bounced between Brad and Suzie.

They nodded. "Of course," Suzie said.

Shelley exhaled and whispered, "Thank you."

An hour later, Shelley slammed the trunk lid down on her Dodge and rechecked the packages in the back seat. She and Suzie worked the afternoon away putting food into plastic containers, stuffing dinners inside insulated sleeves, and gathering cold dishes from the basement. It was nearly three o'clock, another two inches of snow was on the ground, and she needed to get moving. Fortunately, all her deliveries were in town, except for the one errand she needed to run for Brad. She'd offered to pick up the lodge deposit for the day in exchange for him watching the girls this afternoon.

If she didn't get to the bank before five, Brad warned, they could make a night deposit. But she did need to get to the lodge before his assistant manager left for a three-day holiday, and before the roads in the mountain got too bad.

Feeling good about her day and her decision to come back

home, she waved to the porch where Suzie, Petey, and the girls stood in the doorway, then headed out. Smiling, she marveled how yesterday her life was in turmoil. Today, it had done a complete three-sixty. Her heart warmed at the prospect. As she drew closer to the bend in Lake Road that would take her to the lodge, she wavered. If she made her deliveries in town first, then she could stop by the lodge on the way back home.

But then she'd have to go back into Harbor Falls to make the deposit.

Turning right would take her to the lodge. She *could* get the deposit, then backtrack to run all her errands and deliveries in town. But it was early. Would Brad's manager have the deposit ready yet?

Left would take her into Harbor Falls. She glanced at her watch and the sky.

There was plenty of time. People were waiting on their meals. She glanced at the delivery schedule Suzie had typed out for her and knew she had to keep to that schedule. She glanced at the roads. They had been brined the night before and the town snowplow had just gone by. The sky was blue, and nothing was coming down right now.

She turned left and headed downtown.

Chapter Six

"I shouldn't have stayed so long in Asheville."

Learning forward in his seat, Matt stared ahead and realized his were the only wheels breaking through the several inches of snow on the road in front of him. Even if someone had come before him, the rate at which the snow was falling covered everything very quickly. They sure weren't used to snow like this here, and he worried about drivers not knowing how to handle this kind of weather.

The sun had set as he approached Falls Mountain on the southern side. Wet and heavy, the white stuff was piling up. A quick glance to the trees showed weighty branches thick with snow. At least there was no ice. Yet.

"Hope the power holds out," he muttered. "I've got too much to do tonight."

Thankful for his four-wheel drive, he leaned into the steering wheel and concentrated on driving. Soon though, he was mentally ticking off the tasks to do before he could finally relax and get some sleep. He was no Santa, to be sure, but it seemed this night, he might be up all night long. With the back of his Jeep full of presents, he had a couple of hours to get home, wrap some, put together others, and get them all back in the Jeep before heading into Harbor Falls for the midnight candlelight ceremony. If he was lucky, he'd find time for a shower.

He'd tried all day to get his mind off Shelley and his stupid reaction to her at the store. He supposed he'd apologize, eventually, but he didn't want to. He'd put up this stout wall of protection about him for years. He didn't talk about it to anyone, and if someone was insane enough to bring it up, he set them straight right away. The subject of Shelley was off limits. He dealt with it in his own way.

Yeah, by hiding out, you bastard. Is that really dealing?

"Shut up," he said aloud. Chastising himself wasn't going to do any good, either.

Thing was, he didn't know if he wanted to come to terms with the hurt Shelley dealt him. It had dulled, of course, but no one—not one woman he'd encountered since then—had been able to replace her.

That's what scared the hell out of him. He was a strong man, physically, but if he let himself succumb to Shelley, would he survive if she dumped him again? If it somehow didn't work out?

He honestly didn't know.

But no time to dwell on that tonight. He took another hard look at the road before him.

His two older sisters were supposed to be home in time for church. The roads all over were getting icy and slick. That worried him. Could take them longer than expected. It was tradition that if humanly possible, the four of them—his two siblings and his mama—would spend Christmas Eve together at the service. They'd done it since they were kids and their daddy were alive. They'd miss him as always, although he'd been gone for a while.

Once the ceremony was over and the kids were all tucked

into bed at his mama's, he'd unload the Jeep, put some things under the tree and hide others, then hightail it back home for a few hours rest. He knew that his oldest nephew, Brian, nearly ten now, would be calling and waking him way before daylight.

Those plans might have to change. Would he be able to make it back up the mountain to his place after the service?

Hell, it was likely he might not make it back down to the service. Maybe he should turn around and go back to his mother's while he could.

Squinting, he peered through the windshield and increased the rate of swipes his wipers were making. "Seems worse up here," he muttered and frowned while turning onto Lake Road, determined to move forward. His home sat a few miles past old Fall's Lodge and off a dirt road further up. Suited him fine. The more difficult it was to get there, the harder for someone to make the effort.

For good measure, he turned on the radio to the local station. Having spent his afternoon in Asheville, he'd not paid a lot of attention to what was happening in the foothills.

"*Three more inches in the last hour, folks, so we're up to seven here in downtown Harbor Falls and it's just six-thirty. I've heard it's worse in higher country. This stuff is coming down fast, furious, and wet. Forecast says we're not finished yet. Stay in, stay warm, and stay off the roads.*"

"Great." Matt glanced to his cell phone. No calls. He frowned, picked up his radio, patched into the station, and asked for the Chief.

He waited, turned his lights on low beam, and slowed.

The snow shifted into a sleeting mass of ice that blanketed his windshield all too quickly. As he followed the road, now significantly narrowed because of the snow, he began to think that his plans, so thoroughly laid out in his head, were likely to change.

"Matthews?" The crackle met him from the radio.

"Yeah, Chief. Need me down there? Just checking in."

"Didn't want to bother you son, during your time off."

"Yeah but looks bad up here. I'm heading up Lake Road toward home. How is it there?"

"For the most part, fine, power is on, no accidents, people keeping of the streets, but..." The thing crackled and sputtered some more. "are you... lodge?... didn't get... frantic."

"You're breaking up. What?" He crept along, his gaze fixed ahead of him.

"Are you near the lodge?"

"Yes."

"Good. Matthews... sister didn't... home."

What the hell was he saying? Matthews. Suzie?

Matthew's *sister*. Shelley?

"What?" Squinting, his gaze caught and held onto a flash up ahead. Lights.

Something garbled came back.

"Come again, Chief."

"Shelley... missing. Might be... lodge. Didn't make it there."

Lights. Deeper trenches in the snow heading off the edge of the road.

Shelley?

"You hear me Matthews?"

Shit!

A cold iron fist clutched at his chest and squeezed his heart. The lights. The beam. Casting not at him, but straight up into the trees. He braked as easily as he could without sliding off the road. To his right, he could see down over the embankment.

A small car had slid off the road and practically climbed a tall cedar down the hill. If it weren't for the lights, he would have passed it by.

"Gotta go."

Please, Lord, no....

~

S helley sat with her head against the steering wheel, gripping the thing like her last minute on earth depended on it, and panted out breath after breath after breath. Adrenaline shot through her, throbbing in her veins. Crying, she attempted to control her errant breathing and tried really, really hard not to panic.

She wasn't going to be successful on that last part.

Her heart pounded, and fear of what to do next raced through her entire body. Oh God! It all happened so fast, the curve, her tire slipped off the pavement—she couldn't even tell where the freakin' pavement was!—and she'd tipped, slid, and rolled once.

Flipped! She'd flipped the car!

"I don't know what to do," she whimpered. At least she was now upright. "I don't know what to do!"

She was in a tree. A freakin' tree! But thank God, it stopped her from going further down the mountain.

Stupid, stupid, *stupid!* She should have picked up Brad's deposit earlier. She didn't think about the roads being worse at the higher elevation.

Stupid!

She huffed out one huge breath that thoroughly steamed her windshield. "Okay," she whimpered. "Am I hurt?"

No. She didn't think so. Her chest ached from where the seat belt grabbed her and something hit her in the head—maybe her purse?—when she'd rolled.

She glanced to her right. Cell phone. "Where is my..." She leaned to her right.

The car shifted in the tree and she screamed. "Oh, God!" Panic raced through her. "Oh, God!"

Thoughts of her girls ran through her head and she teared again and sobbed. "I want to see my babies!"

Something knocked against her window and she screamed. "Shelley!"

Someone was out there! "Yes!" she screamed and frantically reached for the button to roll down the window. "It won't work! I can't get the window down!"

The voice came again from outside. "Stay calm. Sit still. The windows won't work when the engine is off. Hold on."

The voice. "Okay," she said and slumped into her seat. "Calm, he said. Stay calm."

He shouted again. "I'm trying to see how stable the car is before I try to open the door. Sit still, okay?"

Matt. It was his voice. "Matt?" she screamed. "That you?" Pause.

"Yeah. Just hold on."

She blew a long, slow breath out of her puffed cheeks. Of all people... "Hold on," she whispered. "God, please let him not be so mad at me that he lets me slip on down this mountain..."

Closing her eyes, she tried to breathe evenly, to still her panicky heart. She prayed this would all be over soon.

She heard the latch on the door and risked a glimpse to her left. Slowly the door opened, and framed there in the moonlight, sleet slanting over his face, was Matt. He'd never looked so damn good to her in all her life.

Leaning in, he reached across her—his face way too close to hers—and pushed the latch on her seat belt. She got a whiff of Old Spice. Funny how that scent made tingles shoot through her. He'd been the youngest man she had ever known to wear Old Spice back in high school. She realized she still liked it.

Funny she should think of that now.

He lingered. Looked into her face.

Their gazes caught and every past remembrance of them together shot through her with sudden awareness. At that moment, she realized how much she did not want him to hate her.

"I think your belt is jammed."

She sniffled and a tear fell. "Please cut the damn thing off and get me out of here."

"I don't have anything to cut it. Have to go back to the jeep."

She grabbed his arm. "No! No, please don't leave me, Matt. Please."

"Shelley, this car could slide down the mountain at any moment. We have to get you out."

"I know. I know! But Matt, please don't leave me. I'm begging you. Please don't leave me alone. I can't bear the thought of it."

Matt thought about the irony of that. He didn't want to leave her. Never, ever wanted to leave her all those years ago. It was she who had left, and he who was left alone.

"I won't," he told her. He knew that should the car shift and start to slide again, he'd be there right alongside her. No way would he leave her alone—no matter what happened in their past. "Okay, let's try something."

Her tears were nearly his undoing, and once again, he was sucked into the overpowering feeling of wanting to protect her. Hell, at this point, he only wanted to save her, get her out of this car. He'd deal with any other emotions later.

Go into cop mode, he told himself. Serve. Protect.

He tried hard not to put any more pressure on the car than

he had to, so he didn't lean too heavily into her. The vehicle was rather precariously perched, and he couldn't quite tell what was holding it up, so he didn't want to take any chances and linger.

"Your coat is bulky and you're small. Let me pull the shoulder strap from around you and see if you can take your coat off. Then maybe that will give us enough room to slip you out of the lap belt."

She nodded. "Okay."

He pulled the shoulder belt back and she started peeling out of her coat.

"You're going to be cold."

"I don't care. I'd rather be cold than dead."

He stifled a grin.

"We'll get it back on soon as possible."

She wiggled out of it and he tossed it on the passenger seat.

"Now, I'll hold the lap belt and you..."

The car did a crazy shift to the right. Shelley clutched at his neck about the same time he grabbed her and tried to jerk her up and out. Somehow, in the commotion, the belt gave way, and Brad tumbled out of the car with Shelley landing on top of him.

With a crack and weird buffered scrape of metal against wood, the car tipped to the right and rolled downward.

Shelley buried her face in his chest and let out a huge sob. He wrapped his arms around her and held her tight

"I have you. Don't worry. You're okay."

He heard and felt her crying against his chest. "Thank you," she squeaked out. "For not letting me die." She shook in his arms and he wasn't sure if it was from the cold, or shock.

Matt titled her face and cradled her cheeks in his hands. "I would never let you die, Shelley. My God." He wrapped his arms around her tighter then and held her close. "Let's get out of here," he said after a moment, "You're freezing."

Chapter Seven

S helley welcomed the warmth as Matt wrapped her in his coat and half dragged, half carried her through slush and driving snow up the incline to the Jeep. When they reached his vehicle, he tucked her into the passenger seat, got in on his side, and turned the heater on full blast. She listened as Matt radioed back to the police station and asked the Chief to call Suzie and tell her that Shelley was fine, and that he'd radio again later. After a moment, the chill left her, and she stopped shivering. Somewhat relieved that her family would no longer be worried, she was still bothered by whether the girls knew what had happened. She hoped Suzie had kept that from them. Suddenly, she missed those two chubby faces terribly.

They rode in silence while they climbed in elevation. For a short while, she didn't think about where they were going until they passed the lodge and pulled off the main road— what she could see of the main road anywhere. She wasn't even sure if they were on a road any longer.

"Where are we going?"

Matt didn't respond but concentrated on this driving.

"Matt?"

He finally spoke. "Your seatbelt latched?"

"Yes."

"Good. The road is getting worse."

She stared ahead and burrowed into his lined suede jacket. It smelled like him and she breathed deep. It was a comfort. "We're not going back to Harbor Falls. Are we?" She angled her gaze his way. He stared straight ahead, peering down the road. She noticed that even without his coat, he showed no outward appearance of being cold. In fact, he showed no outward appearance of anything, emotion included.

"No," he finally answered.

"Then where?"

"Can't go back down, the roads are too bad. No way to turn the Jeep around safely."

"I asked you where, not why."

He didn't respond.

It was Christmas Eve and she was going to be away from her children. Tears stung her eyes. Tomorrow would be Christmas morning. And here she was, stuck in God-knows-where with her moody ex-boyfriend.

A sob caught in her throat. Dammit, she would not let him see her cry anymore. Every time he had seen her the past day or so, she was crying. At least she was alive. That should be consolation enough, and there would be many more Christmas Eves with her children.

She should count her lucky stars.

She should thank *him*. Had she?

"Matt, Th—"

The vehicle lurched to the right, and then back to the left. She didn't finish her words and grasped at the door handle. He turned the Jeep and she looked in front of them. A security light shone through the falling snow and rested on a small cabin nestled in some pines not far away. The building was barely visible.

Uncertain about this turn of events, Shelley looked at him, and finally he met her gaze with a look of determination.

"Matt, where are you taking me?"

He didn't blink an eye. "Home," he said, "Where I should have taken you years ago."

Something both physical and emotional hit her in the gut right then. It almost took her breath away.

~

The second those words were out of his mouth, Matt regretted them. His gaze locked with Shelley's eyes and he watched as a flurry of emotion swept through them. They misted slightly and her lips parted. She shook her head a little from side to side.

Her words were soft spoken, hushed. "Matt, I... I don't know what to say. What do you mean?"

Matt watched Shelley's chest rise and fall, her breathing a little unsteady. He broke the connection and glanced to her hands, knit into a knot on her lap. He was an idiot. The words shouldn't have come out of his mouth like that, but they were the words in his head. Sometimes he needed a brain check. Now was one of those times. He studied her face again. This time she was searching his eyes for answers.

"Matt?"

He reached for her hands, clasped them quickly, and then released them. In the same moment, he physically straightened himself as much as possible to provide some distance. "I shouldn't have said that. Just forgot it."

She grasped his shirtsleeve. "No Matt. Tell me."

The emotion raking through him with the tug of her fingers and her seeking eyes was nearly his undoing. He wanted to haul her up close and kiss her with all the pent-up hormonal passion of the teenage boy he was when he first kissed her. He wanted to sink himself into her core and make her his again. He wanted to carry her over the threshold of his cabin and never let her go. Ever.

But he wouldn't.

He reached for the placket of his jacket and pulled it tight snugly around her. "We need to get inside. Hold this tight and pull it up around your neck and head. I'll come around and help you to the porch and up the steps."

He avoided looking into her eyes until the very last second, and then he did. Her feathered lashes fluttered and framed her doe-eyed stare into his face.

She whispered, "Matt, I'm so confused."

Her breath was soft against his cheek. Nodding, he replied, "That makes two of us, sweetheart."

They made it into the cabin by holding onto each other and tripping their way through the growing drifts. Soon, they were inside. Shelley stood in the entry, slithered out of his coat, and held it protectively in front of her. Matt tramped his feet on a rug, pulled off his boots and set them by the door, then moved to the fireplace across the room. He bent to stoke the fire burning there.

In awe, Shelley glanced about.

Not huge by any means, the cabin was warm and cozy, with a clear-cut male influence. The stone fireplace was the focal point, looming large and masculine beneath exposed rough-hewn beams. The walls were bare wood. It looked to be a true log cabin. A dark brown leather couch with a couple of heavy afghans draped over it sat facing the fireplace. Oversized armchairs balanced each side.

She spanned the larger room and noticed an open kitchen to the left, complete with a small breakfast nook tucked back into the corner. It appeared well equipped with all the necessary appliances, and well kept. To the right was a half-closed wooden door to another room. His bedroom?

She was sure she would never find that out.

His statement earlier still rang in his ears. *Home. Where I should have taken you years ago.* What the hell did that mean? He didn't have this cabin all those years ago.

No. He built one here for himself. And a fine one.

Without her.

She didn't want to think about it.

Well, yes, maybe she did. They were young and idealistic years ago. Just out of high school and talking of a future home together. They had even sketched out the plans for a cabin in the woods, with kids and puppies and....

It was what she wanted then. He wasn't ready for that responsibility yet. They were too young and they both were looking at colleges. But they liked the dream and talked of it often.

Suddenly she knew why that ache landed deep in her tummy a moment ago. Reality. He had built their cabin, even though she had dumped him.

Why?

Her gut clutched. She knew exactly why. *Don't think about that right now, Shelley. Not yet.*

So, while he fiddled with the fire she concentrated on the room about her. Yes, that was safe. Furniture, fireplace, things on the wall. What drew her in was the essence of wood. Not only the beams and the walls, but also the intricately detailed carvings that sat about the room. Her gaze landed on first one item, then another. A small black bear cub lay on its back on an end table. An eagle perched majestically on the mantle. A mother deer and twin fawns quietly grazed on a shelf. A carved picture of the mountains, with layers of dimension and depth, hung on the wall next to the fireplace. A set of wooden bowls on the counter graced a lake scene.

"Oh, my," she whispered.

Matt looked up and her gaze fell to meet his. He stood and ran his hands down his thighs. Finally, he moved toward her. "Here, let me take the coat. Slip out of your shoes, okay?"

She nodded and did what he asked, not quite sure why she was so taken aback with Matt's home. She remembered when they were kids he used to whittle all the time. One time he made her a small heart and put it on a chain. In fact, she still kept it in her jewelry box.

His gaze met hers as he reached for the coat.

"Matt, did you do all this?"

He pursed his lips and glanced about. "Yes."

"All of it?"

His gaze circled the interior of the cabin. "Yes. I had help with the cabin, of course, but some of the wooden furniture and all of the carvings are mine." He looked back to her.

"Matt, it's all...breathtaking." She reached for the bear cub. "May I?" He nodded and she lifted it closer to her face. "You are very talented."

Slipping the coat over a barstool, he glanced off and perused his cabin, then back to her. "I had time on my hands." He shoved his hands in his pockets. "Bought a little patch of land before Brad Matthews bought the lodge property."

Finally, Shelley found her feet and moved further into the room. She knew she should be thinking more pertinent things, rather than how Matt had occupied his time for the past few years—like how in the world they managed not to argue thus far, and when they would be able to get back down the mountain—but for some odd reason, she was spellbound, and in awe of Matt's work.

She turned toward him and caught him staring at her. "Matt, I..."

A muffled crack sounded from somewhere outside, then a lengthy scrape against the side of the cabin. The lights flickered and Shelley kept her gaze on his face. He looked away but she still watched as the lights came back on, briefly flickered again, and finally, thrust them into darkness.

Chapter Eight

M att swore under his breath but was secretly glad the lights went out. With Shelley standing there in his cabin, his heart pounded, and he wasn't quite sure how he would get through the evening. Now, perhaps, in the dark, he might be able to survive a little better.

Although he really did not want to lose power, the cover of darkness felt safe. He knew the fireplace would keep them warm and he had enough food and water to sustain them until this storm passed. He had a backup generator but didn't relish the idea of traipsing out back to the shed in this storm to kick it into action. If he had to, he would, but for the moment, he preferred staying put.

"Stay still," he told Shelley and started toward her. "I think we can see well enough with the fire. Maybe it will come back on in a minute." He doubted it, sure that a low-hanging branch weighted down too heavy with snow, had ripped the power line from the side of the house. Easy enough fix, but not tonight. He'd see to it tomorrow but knowing that tomorrow was Christmas day, and given the conditions of the mountain road, getting a power truck up here seemed unlikely.

Matt grasped her elbow. "Let's sit by the fire." He wanted to say, *We need to talk,* but didn't.

He led her there and settled her on the raised hearth.

"This feels good," she said. "Maybe the heat will dry my jeans."

Dammit, he hadn't noticed that her clothes were wet. Glancing down at himself, he was in the same boat. "Hell, I'm sorry. I wasn't thinking. Let me see if I can find us something dry to put on."

He left her by the fire and trekked off to his bedroom. Thoughts flew through his head like a house afire. One glance back as he entered his bedroom door and his heart began a slow thrum. He left the door open so partial light from the fire would give some illumination in the darkened room.

Shelley was here in his cabin. Not his plan, yet it had happened, and he had to deal with it. But how?

He found his chest of drawers in the low light and fumbled through a couple of drawers. Hell, he had nothing small enough to fit her, did he?

Finally, he brought up a smaller pair of jogging pants and an old high school sweatshirt. Smiling, he wondered if she'd remember it. He quickly changed himself, grabbed the clothes for her, and stopped abruptly at his bedroom door to observe her silhouette against the fire.

The flame flickered over her blond tresses, setting off a fiery halo around her head. She threaded her fingers through her hair, fluffing to dry the length. His breath caught in his throat.

He knew at that moment that he still loved her. Had never stopped.

Hell, he'd always known he'd loved her but had kept his heart locked and safe while she was gone. He hadn't let his emotions rest on that fact for any length of time over the years. He'd been working on "getting over her" as he'd been told to do by his guy friends, and an occasional date, and his family.

But he'd never, truly, been able to get over her. She'd lingered in the back of his heart. No one ever come close to touching that part of his heart and he'd guarded it and kept it safe—just in case she ever did come back into his life.

And now here she was. Back. In the place they'd dreamed about for their future. Where he'd dreamed she might someday come back to.

But could he trust her?

Could he trust himself?

He wasn't so damned sure he could guard his heart now that she was here.

Had only he'd been ready to be a husband, to give her what she wanted and needed all those years ago—a home, family, children, the goddamned picket fence and all that— then maybe she wouldn't have run off into some other man's willing and able arms. Some guy who was what she thought she wanted at the time.

But no, he hadn't been ready then, couldn't handle those responsibilities. They were too young. He wasn't ready to take on what his father had at a young age and had died trying to keep intact. They'd grown up poor and his father worked his fingers to the bone to support them. Without a college degree, he'd labored hard. Even at nineteen, Matt knew he'd be damned if he would do the same thing for his future family. His path was different. He would go to college, get the degree, and provide for his future family without struggling.

Back then, he'd desperately wanted to give Shelley everything. She was the only woman he wanted.

But she couldn't wait... And he wouldn't change his plans.

Suddenly, he realized there was nothing he could do about the past, but he damn well could make some alterations to his future. Their future. If he could only let go of the hurt, the lack of trust.

Physically, he was a strong man. Could his heart be strong enough to risk the emotion again?

~

"See if these will work. I'm sure they are much too big but at least you'll be dry and warm."

His soft voice came to her on a whisper. Shelley's gaze drifted up to meet his. He thrust something toward, her but she didn't see what. Clothes perhaps? All she could see was the fire reflecting in his deep brown eyes looking down at her.

Warm, inviting, lonely.

She'd been such a fool. Young and naive. And for the few minutes he was gone, she had stared into the fireplace and realized just that.

She didn't regret marrying Cliff and she loved her girls to no end. But she did regret all the pain and hurt she'd caused so many people.

Swallowing hard over a growing lump in throat, she rose and stepped closer to Matt. Gathering up the clothes he held out to her, she clutched them to her chest but never let her stare waver from his. She peered deeper.

"I know I've said this once, but I'm going to say it again. I'm so sorry, Matt," she whispered. "For everything."

Something broke in his expression and she waited while his gaze played over her face, searching, probing. It landed on her lips, and then lifted to catch her stare again.

An overwhelming desire to rush forward, lift her face to his and kiss him came over her. She tamped it back. No, she could not do that. He was angry with her. Hated her. She was stuck with him here and who knew what his reaction might—

He reached out and skimmed his fingertips along her

cheek and jawline, and a burst of pleasure sped through her, confusing her even more.

"Matt..." she squeaked out.

In one swift moment, he grasped the clothing from her hands, tossed them away, and hauled her up against him. His mouth came down hard on hers and she gasped at the sensation. Firm and determined, he kissed her thoroughly, his hands at her back holding her against his chest, his lips playing over hers, his tongue searching for more.

The unleashed passion boiling up in her was like an answer to a long-awaited prayer—an urgent yearning suppressed and set free. It was like a piece of her heart had been put back in her chest—a piece that she didn't know was missing until that very moment. Heat welled up until she thought her chest would burst.

She was kissing Matt. *Matt!* Not her high school boyfriend, but Matt, the man. The one she'd left behind. And unless she was mistaken, he was hungry for more.

But... But what could this lead to? Where could it go?

Those thoughts dissipated as his mouth left her lips and trailed lazily down her neck in a sensual rhythm. A deep sigh escaped his lips. She melted against him.

"Let's get you out of these wet clothes." His voice was deep and raspy against the crook of her neck and shoulder.

Shelley pulled back and searched his face. She wondered if he could read her question. Should they?

With a forefinger on her lips, he shook his head. "Don't... talk. Let's..."

This time she was the one who sprung forward and met his lips in a sensual embrace. No words. No thoughts. Only lips communicating with lips, bodies speaking to bodies.

They tumbled to the floor in front of the fireplace, landing on a plush rug. Matt shoved the coffee table out of the way and pulled an afghan down from the sofa. She lay on her back, looking up at him as he cradled her close and stared into her eyes.

The fire made the ambience perfect. Soft flickers of flame wrapped them in a sultry glow. Perfect, *perfect...*

But it couldn't be perfect, could it?

That second came and went as he reached for the placket of her shirt and unbuttoned in a lazy, southerly direction. His fingertips grazed the tender skin of her breasts, along her tummy, all the way down. His gaze never left hers.

She shivered at his touch and the fire within gathered to meet the one raging beside her in the hearth.

She wanted him. After all this time. And he...he wanted her, too?

Yes. He did.

Matt pushed the shirt off her shoulders, and she lifted slightly while he removed and tossed it aside. The heat from the fireplace warmed her but as soon as he placed his palm over one of her breasts and kneaded, she knew that fire was insignificant compared to the one burning deep in her belly.

The next seconds were filled with a frenetic tangle of limbs and peeling off damp clothing, searching for and taking care of a condom, frenzied breaths, and frantic kisses.

"Your skin is so cold, Shelley. Come here," he rasped, and covered her body with his. "Let me warm you up."

She nodded against his lips, fused with hers.

Their bodies came together, and Shelley knew that the skin-to-skin contact they shared had never felt so good. Scorching against her, his body covered hers and she opened for him. She relished in the feel of his length, the caress against her folds, and realized that this coming together of their bodies for the first time in years was far superior to simple skin-to-skin contact. She ached for him and eagerly took him. His body rocked into hers and they melded together despite the years of anguish and hurt.

From that moment on, any doubt, any question, any insane thought that she shouldn't be exactly where she was at this moment in time, vanished.

❧

With a deep inhale, Matt breathed in Shelley's scent as he sank into her. Dizzy with the sensation, he settled his face against her hair and stilled for only a second as he reveled in the feel of being inside her again. His thoughts didn't linger except for one.

This was right. Yes. This was right...

He thrust deeper as she whimpered and urged him on, her legs wrapped around him, her fingertips grazing his back.

He wanted to savor, linger, slowly bring her to climax, and then spill himself inside her. His body took over, however, and did the opposite. As did hers. She gasped and clenched her thighs around him as he moved in and out. He growled in her ear. He couldn't stop pumping. Filling her. Feeling her velvet insides pulling him deeper. Wouldn't stop. No. This beautiful thing that was them, together, moved him in ways that took him from the past to the present and back again.

"Oh...oh, Matt...."

His whispered name on her lips was nearly his undoing.

Hold on. Hold on...

She trembled and gasped in short pants, digging her fingernails into his back, her legs clamping him to her, while she shuddered beneath him. The sounds, her whimpers of satisfaction, gratified him. He'd always loved giving her pleasure. Simultaneously, he groaned his eruptive release and pushed one last time into her, her quaking body settling around him like a caress.

Melting into her, he wasn't quite sure where he ended, and she began.

Chapter Nine

S helley blinked herself awake and stared into a smoldering fire. The embers were red and glowing, pulsating against the semi-darkness of the room— much like her body thrummed in the night each time Matt made hot and steamy love to her. The first time they came together was fast and unrestrained. The second was slow and deliberate, making up for years of neglect.

Now, as morning closed in, the room was chilly and the fire dying. She hoped that was not a metaphor for things to come. Few words were said while they made love and Shelley knew that today, the dialogue they had avoided during the night would have to happen.

Matt spooned her from behind as they faced the fireplace. He'd wrapped her in a cocoon made of his body and the afghan after their last, exhausting love-making session. His breathing was even, with deep easy breaths, warm against her neck. His arm lay heavy across her shoulder and chest, holding her close.

It would be easy to get lost in this. Waking up with him

every morning. Feeling safe and secure and protected, here in this cabin.

No. It was a fantasy. Couldn't happen.

Could it?

Sighing, she squeezed her eyes tight. No, she was vulnerable. It was too soon. He really didn't want her. They had succumbed to... Something physical. Need. Want. A reaction from the accident. Right?

This wasn't real. This couldn't last.

Could it?

Shivering, she pulled the afghan up closer to her chin, unsure if it was an effort to keep warm, or ward off negative thoughts that tempted to invade her momentary bliss.

≈

"Cold?"

Awake for several minutes, Matt avoided stirring, not wanting to wake her. Dammit, that wasn't the truth. It was more primal than that. He didn't want to move, to break contact with her body. Having Shelley nestled up against him was like a balm to his aching heart, a salve for his soul.

He didn't want her to leave. He didn't know how to ask her to stay. Or if he should.

"No, not really," she said quietly.

With his eyes closed, he tightened his hold on her and pictured them together in his mind's eye. What would it be like, to wake up like this when they were old and gray? "I'll get up in a minute and stoke the fire back to life," he mumbled.

He'd rather stoke her fire, but now, as daylight teased through the windows, he didn't feel as confident about that as he did in the dark of night.

"Take your time," she whispered. "I'm warm enough."

Again, she sighed deeply, and he wondered what that

meant. He'd like to think it was a sigh of contentment, although not convinced that it was. "Me, too."

Quiet settled around them, interrupted only with an intermittent crackle and hiss from the fireplace.

"Has the snow stopped?" She sounded tentative, uncertain.

"Not sure."

Sitting up on an elbow, he glanced at the kitchen window and then back to Shelley. The afghan fell to her waist and his gaze trailed over the curve of her naked back. He debated massaging her shoulders and trailing his fingers over her satin skin until she gave in and let him take her again, but he didn't act on it. She didn't turn toward him either, instead continuing to stare into the fire.

Awkward.

Instead, he settled behind her. His palm lay loose over her chest and he was certain he felt the subtle beating of her heart. "I think the snow has stopped. I'll check on the road conditions in a minute."

He felt the nod of her head. She said nothing.

"Are you okay?" He whispered, not certain how to begin the conversation he knew needed to be had.

She didn't immediately answer, still looking intently ahead. After a moment, she turned in his arms toward him. A ray of morning light slanted in the window across her face. She looked dewy and soft, her eyes a bit misty, her face lined with worry.

"I don't know how I am."

Matt traced the outline of her face with his forefinger, and then crooked it under her chin. She trembled as he stroked her tender skin with a light touch of his thumb while searching her face. "Guess we're in a weird place, huh?"

"Sort of. You hate me, Matt. I—."

He put a finger on her lips and huffed out a breath. "Shelley, if I hated you I couldn't have made love to you last night like I did. Like *we* did."

Her eyes shut tight. Tiny crinkles shot out from the corners.

"Matt..." she sucked in a breath and exhaled, "I don't know... We..."

"Shelley, look at me."

She did, her blue eyes questioning.

"I don't hate you."

"You told me to stay away from you."

"That was yesterday. I was mad."

"You've been mad at me for a long time. I hurt you. Bad."

He paused, careful with his next words. She was right. The hurt, even though for a while last night had lessened, still hadn't gone away. He didn't want to lie, and he didn't want to sugarcoat. "Yes. I've been mad at you for a long time. You did hurt me."

"That doesn't go away overnight."

"No. No, you're right."

"But you could still make love to me?"

"I... Shelley, yes."

She stared at him. "How can you turn it off and on like that?" Her voice rose.

"Shelley, you were finally here, in my house. So many things were going through my head... I wanted—"

"You wanted sex."

Stunned, he pulled back. "No, it wasn't like that. I wanted you."

Her head shook and he wasn't sure she heard anything he said. Not really.

"I didn't think," she began. "I... I didn't think, Matt. I let you, us.... I didn't think of the consequences. And now..."

Shit. What was she saying? "And now what?"

She pushed away and drew the afghan up to her chest.

"Maybe... Oh, Matt. Maybe this was a mistake. I just don't know..."

Dammit! How in hell could he let himself get sucked in again? He sat up, tossing the afghan off him and fully onto her. Standing now, he found his sweatpants and stepped into them. "Never mind, Shelley. I get it. You just woke up with the realization you had 'oh shit' sex."

"What?"

He raked his fingers through his hair and paced. "You know, 'oh shit' sex. You wake up, realize you're in bed with someone, and you're not sure why you did it, and you think, 'oh shit, what the hell have I done?'"

Shelley sat straight up. "Matt, that's not what I was thinking! I would never think that about you. It's just that we are starting over. It's very soon, and... Oh hell."

He waved her off. "Never mind. I get it."

Her eyes widened. "Get what?"

He needed a change of venue and fast. Shit. They were snowbound. Were they still? What were the roads like? His brain spun with confusion. Could he get out of here? Didn't matter. He needed out of the house, now, away from Shelley. To think.

To put up that guard around his heart again, perhaps.

A quick glimpse to the hearth told him they were low on firewood. "I'm going to get wood. While I'm out, I'll check on the weather and radio down to Harbor Falls to see about the roads."

With a brisk turn toward him, she wrapped the afghan around her and stood. "Do you think we can get out of here today?"

The look on her face held a sense of urgency.

"In that much of a hurry to leave?"

Her brows knit and she glanced toward the door. "No, Matt. I—"

He stomped away, then halted and spun around, and her words cut off. Laughing aloud, he interrupted. "Of course, you are in a hurry to leave. That's what you're good at, Shelley. Leaving. Why should I expect anything different?" His stare bit into her eyes. "Don't worry. I'll get you off this goddamned mountain. I wouldn't want you to stick around for too long and get, well, attached or anything."

Immediately, her eyes welled up and she lifted her chin in defiance. He knew that gesture well. She used to do it when they were kids and he'd pissed her off. Dammit, but he didn't want or need to see it again because it has always melted his resistance like butter on a corn cob.

He'd hurt her. Hadn't meant to.

Maybe it was better this way. If she hated him, it would easier all the way around.

"It's Christmas morning, Matt," she bit out. "I was thinking about my girls."

He deflated. Feeling like heel, he swiped at his sweatshirt and picked it up. With the same motion, he tucked his heart back deep in his chest, safe and secure. Why the hell had it let it out? This was impossible, and the sooner they both realized it, the better off they'd both be.

"Of course. Your girls."

"They are important to me. Matt, they are all I have."

Of course.

Dammit. His brain swirled with uncertainty. With emotion he couldn't pin down. Fear. Trust, or the lack of it. Worry. Love?

He clenched and unclenched his fists, trying to gain some semblance of control. "Of course, Shelley. I'm sorry. I understand that you need to get to your girls. They want their mother, too, on Christmas morning. I get it."

"Okay..." She bit her lip. "Matt, this is all a mess and we need to talk about it. All of it."

He nodded. "Yes. But not now. Let's get you back to your family, and honestly, I need to see if I can get to mine. Looks like we both have obligations."

After a moment, she agreed. "Okay, Matt. Okay."

Somehow, he didn't think it was okay. Dammit, he wasn't good at this relationship thing. Not good at all. He'd screwed them up years ago with his lofty dreams and goals. What made him think he wouldn't screw it up again? He jerked the sweatshirt over his head while she watched. Her gaze trailed his every move. He really didn't want to look at her, wrapped up in his afghan, naked underneath....

Couldn't. His resolve might crumble.

Striding toward where his coat and boots rested, he donned them with a brief backward glance.

"I'll be back in a few minutes. Make yourself at home."

Immediately, he regretted those words. *Home*. This cabin would never be a home for Shelley. There was too much bad history between them. He doubted either of them had the energy or the inclination to turn all the negatives around.

He knew he didn't.

Yanking open the cabin door, he stepped out onto his snow-drifted stoop and looked at his Jeep. "Dammit all to hell." He'd have to dig out but dig out he would. No way could he spend one more night alone in this cabin with Shelley. He was too confused, too...something.

The door slammed shut behind him.

～

Staring at the large wood door, Shelley stood by the fireplace unmoving, sniffing away tears as she contemplated the symbolism of that slamming door. It stood solid and unmoving between them, like the chasm of hurt and betrayal she was darned certain would never go away.

It was all her fault. All of it.

She had caused the pain for Matt and everyone else she loved when she stupidly made the one decision that would haunt her for the rest of her life

Possibly, that one decision was going to take away one of the best things that could have happened to her.

Matt.

It was over. No hopes and dreams here, so she might as well get used to it.

With a cleansing exhale, she played a lazy gaze over the room, landing on each carving Matt had done, taking in the loving care he put into each detail. She perused the rough-hewn beams, and her search lingered on the precise layering of chinks between the cedar logs. Closing her eyes, she imagined Matt up here working on this cabin in his spare time—nights, weekends, any time he could muster. That was the way he was.

Determined. Goal-oriented.

Again, she sniffled, but even with her eyes closed, she couldn't stop the tears.

She'd screwed up.

But the past was the past. She had to move forward and let Matt go. And if he knew what was good for him, he needed to let her go, too.

She opened her eyes. Yes. That was exactly what had to happen.

Turning, she glimpsed at her clothes scattered near the hearth and prayed they were dry. As she reached for them, her gaze landed on the plush rug, the coffee table pushed askew, the indentation where they had lain in the night—all evidence of their lovemaking.

A pang settled in her tummy.

She dismissed it. Another memory. It meant nothing.

"Liar," she whispered, swiping away a lingering tear. "It means everything."

But she would not dwell on it. There was no hope. She wasn't worthy of Matt. He was a good guy and he was confused as much as she, and she wanted the best for him.

That wouldn't happen with her. She was not the best thing for him.

Snatching up her clothes, she tossed the afghan aside.

"Get dressed and be ready to leave as soon as he gets back." That was her only defense. Get the hell out. Yes, Matt nailed her with that earlier. She was good at leaving.

So be it.

Chapter Ten

The silence in the Jeep split the cool climate between them like a razor-sharp icicle hanging from a rooftop. Although unspoken words hung in the air, neither of them dared break the silence. Matt supposed they'd each come to the same conclusion.

Give it up. This wasn't going anywhere.

When he had returned to the cabin earlier, he found her dressed and ready to leave, sitting on the hearth and staring at the dying embers.

Appropriate.

Ready to go.

Saying nothing, he changed into dry clothing. Once dressed, he motioned toward the door and led her to his vehicle. The hardest part was getting out of his short dirt road. After that, the Jeep plowed through the six inches or so of snow on the mountain road with cautious ease, the morning sun already having melted some of it. He was thankful this side of the mountain faced east.

He sensed a change in Shelley the moment he stepped

inside the door. There was something final about that sensation. He didn't question but accepted.

It was over. Finally. Maybe now he could move on.

That was the way it remained as they drove the five miles or so back toward Lake Road. They passed the lodge and the place where Shelley's car slid off the road. With a peripheral glance, he saw her look down the mountain. Her chest lifted and lowered with a deep sigh.

"Thank you for saving me," she whispered, still looking out the window.

He wanted to say many things then, like, *How could I not save you? I love you*, but he didn't. "You're welcome," he responded, his stare fixed on the road.

That was their only exchange until they turned into Suzie's drive. Shelley sat up straighter as she watched the front door of her sister's house. She scooted a little closer to the edge of her seat, as far as the seatbelt would allow, and clutched at the door handle.

Eager to get the hell out of here.

He stopped the Jeep, and everything froze. Finally, he turned and found her peering back at him, her eyes glazed with tears.

"I know you will probably never forgive me, Matt," she said softly, "but I am truly sorry. You have to forget about it, and me, and move on."

Well, there it was, the final blow. Confirmation that there was not a snowball's chance in hell that they would ever come to terms.

He held her stare for way too long and her tears spilled over. At once, he softened toward her a little. Giving her a quick nod, he hoped she understood what that meant because he didn't want to have to say it out loud.

He would forget. He would let it go. Let her go.

The lifting of the door handle latch broke the silence and

Shelley turned away. In an instant, she was out of the truck, picking her way through the snow, and toward the house.

Make sure she gets inside and then leave.

In truth, he wanted to linger, catch the morning rays glinting off her hair, take in her determined step across the porch, wait and see if perhaps she might give him a backward glance.

She didn't.

Suzie opened the door and within a half-second, Shelley was whisked inside.

He exhaled, steaming up his windshield.

Abruptly, the front door opened again,

and his heart picked up a cadence. Suzie took a step out onto the porch and waved. A thank you, he was certain. Huffing out one last cleansing breath, an attempt to still his racing heart, he waved back and put the Jeep into reverse.

"Put it to rest, Branson. It's over."

It was time to get to his own family. Where he belonged.

Where his heart was safe.

≈

"Me! Me! It's my turn Uncle Bad!"

Shelley watched Karly jump up and down in front of her uncle and beg for his hands. He grasped both of her tiny palms in his while she climbed flat-footed up his legs and thighs and turned a flip, grinning all the while.

"Again! Again!"

Brad tossed a look of feigned despair at Shelley. "Your kids are wearing me out!"

"He loves every minute of it," Suzie said from her right. "It's good practice for him to manage multiple kids."

"Oh?" Shelley wondered what that last part meant. "Are you indicating anything, Suzie?"

She watched her sister toss her husband a quick smile, then back to her. "No indication of anything, dear sister. We're just *practicing*."

Shelley sniggered. "I'll just let that stay right there."

"Good idea." Suzie turned back to her work.

All three children—Katie, Karly and Petey—giggled and bounced on the floor, amidst wads of Christmas wrapping paper and scattered toys, in front of him. "More!" Petey said.

Shelley watched as Brad scooped his son into his arms and sank into an overstuffed chair behind him, propping his legs on an ottoman. "I'm pooped."

The girls started to climb.

"Katie. Karly. Come here. Uncle Bad is tired." Shelley motioned for her girls and they came running. She gathered them onto her lap.

Suzie leaned closer and whispered. "And we definitely do not want to wear Uncle Bad out, he needs to save some of that energy for me."

Shelley looked into her sister's eyes and caught the twinkle. She laughed aloud.

Grinning, Suzie hugged her. "Well, that was nice. That's the first laugh I've heard from you all day.

Glancing off with a frown, Suzie chided herself. She thought she had hidden her sadness pretty darn well. Seeing her parents earlier made her temporarily forget about Matt and the previous night. She was lost in the moment of hugging and crying and apologizing—seemed she was always apologizing lately—and focused only on the events happening right in front of her. She thought she'd pulled it off.

Obviously, her sister could see through her ploy.

"Oh, I beg to differ," she replied. "I'm pretty sure I laughed earlier when the kids were opening their presents and Petey got tangled in the ribbon. And what about when Daddy slurped up that banana pudding and it spurted on his shirt? I'm sure I laughed then."

Suzie shook her head. "No. You smiled a little. But no laughter."

She waved her off. "Ridiculous." She thought for a moment. "What about when Brad brought the puppy in for the girls? I know I laughed watching the kids all-a-tumble on the floor with the pup. That was pretty funny when the pup took off with Petey's sock."

Again, Suzie shook her head. "No, you barely smiled then."

Smirking, Shelley exhaled hard. "Well, all right. Maybe not."

Chaos ensued. The girls rolled off her lap and wrestled with the puppy again on the floor. Petey climbed all over his dad trying to avoid getting tickled. Joan Hart, their mother, scurried about picking up stray ribbon and wrapping paper. Her father fiddled with the stereo, attempting to find a radio station with Christmas music that fit his taste. He was tired of *Rock Around the Christmas Tree.*

"What happened, Shelley? Up at Matt's cabin?"

Surprised that she would ask—or even sense that she should ask—Shelley looked away. She didn't want to meet Suzie's stare, and felt every iota of its intensity on her face. "Nothing. Nothing that I want to talk about right now, anyway."

Suzie remained quiet and pressed her hand into her sister's palm.

"I just want to sit here and enjoy my family," Shelley whispered.

Suzie squeezed. "Yeah," she said, "Look at us. We're pretty darned good-looking to be so dysfunctional, aren't we?"

Shelley bit her lip and looked at her sister. Both women

burst out laughing. She laughed so hard she hoped no one noticed her tears.

~

Across town, Matt stood in his mother's kitchen drying dishes while his two sisters took a smoke out on the deck, and his nieces and nephews played with their toys in the den. He hated that both of his siblings smoked, but at least they didn't do it in front of the kids.

His mother handed him the turkey platter and said, "I hear Shelley is back in town."

He took the platter but didn't say a word, only gave a half-nod. Silence drifted between them for a moment.

Then his mother added, "The last thing I want for you is to hurt again, Matthew."

He could agree with that statement. His mother dipped a pan into the dishwater and silently washed the dish for a few long seconds. Matt set the platter on the counter.

Turning, his mother stopped the washing motions and rested her hands on the edge of the sink. "Yes, the last thing I want for you is more hurt, but I also want to you to face this situation, Matthew. You either need to get on with your life without Shelley, or you need to go after her."

Little do you know, Mom....

"Do you know what I mean?"

"I know exactly what you mean."

"Then what will you do?" Her eyes searched his as only a mother's could. He could see the love and caring in them, and he knew she only wanted what was best for him.

"I already did that, Mom, and it didn't work out."

She took the dishtowel from him and dried her hands. "What are you talking about?"

Crossing his arms over his chest, he leaned a hip into the

counter. "I went after her again. Last night. Shelley got stranded up by the lodge and I took her home with me for the night. I dropped her off at Suzie's before I came here."

A hint of a smile broke across her face. "And?"

He inhaled deep and let the breath out slower. "It didn't work. I went after her and she told me to let it go, Mom. So that's what I'm doing."

His mother's smile morphed into pursed lips. "Not exactly what I wanted to hear. I'm disappointed in her. I thought perhaps..."

Matt stepped closer. "It's not Shelley, mom. It's me. I gave it a shot, it didn't work. I'm fine now, or I will be. I needed this to happen so I could get past everything. Past her. Don't worry about me, okay? I'm fine."

He hugged her then and she hugged him back. "I love you son and want you to be happy."

He nodded. "I promise. I'm happy. Or I will be soon."

She broke away to investigate his face, cupped his cheek in a palm, and smiled. "I know you will be. I had high hopes—back then and now. I've never seen another young couple like the two of you, so much in love. I was sure that love of yours could stand the tests of time and that eventually, even after everything, you would get back together."

"I had hoped that too, Mom. It's just not the reality."

"You still love her, Matthew. I can still see it in your eyes when you talk about her."

He sighed. "Mom, I'll never stop loving her. I just have to figure out how to love her and live without her."

She clasped him close again and hugged him tight, like only a concerned mother could.

Chapter Eleven

Thankful for the busy day, Shelley sat on the edge of her bed some hours later and blew out a heavy sigh. For a variety of reasons, she'd fought tears all day. The children were beautiful and funny, so full of life. She mourned the fact that Cliff would never see them grow up and become young women.

So grateful that her parents were forgiving and loving people, she'd choked back tears more than once just looking at them, watching them enjoy her children. When her father came close to tearing up himself, she'd almost lost it, but held on. And Suzie—her compassionate sister Suzie who loved her unconditionally and should probably hate her—was always there with open, loving arms. She owed her so much and didn't deserve the kindness her sister had shown her.

There truly was nothing better than family. At least her family. Of course, Harbor Falls had built a tradition on family, which was why coming home was both hard, and wonderful, all at once.

Shelley wondered what Matt was doing today with his family.

He had filtered in and out of her thoughts most of the day but by dinnertime, she had mastered pushing him out of her head.

Well, not really. She'd only told herself that. Pretending was a skill she had acquired over the past few years.

Now, in the quiet of the evening, the cacophony of Christmas laid to rest and her children tucked into bed, her mind longed to still itself—to empty of the chaos of the holidays and her homecoming and finally relax.

But when her mind did turn off, he was there.

Matt was in her head. She could taste him on her lips. Feel him in the palms of her hands.

He was tucked firmly in her heart.

Twisting toward the bed pillows, she tugged at the quilt and slipped between the cool sheets. The pillowcase was crisp and sweet smelling, and she wanted to bury herself in the comfort. Just twenty-four hours earlier, she'd lain on her same side, looking into a rolling fire, with Matt spooning her back. Now, she lay alone, looking into the small night lamp on her bedside table, and finally, the tears flowed.

She wasn't sure if they were tears of joy, loss, or relief. Perhaps they were simply a manifest of the release she needed to allow herself.

A soft, quick knock sounded on her door and without waiting for a response, Suzie slipped inside.

"Suzie?" Shelley pushed up on an elbow and knew Suzie could see her tear-stained face. No use to hide it now.

Her big sister approached, and Shelley sat fully up. Suzie sat and embraced her, circling her close. Shelley continued to cry.

"Did Matt hurt you?" Suzie asked. "I mean, not physically. Matt isn't that kind. But with words?"

She shook her head. "No, of course not."

"Was he angry?"

"Not too much. Some."

"Hm." Suzie stroked her hair and Shelley kept her face buried on her sister's shoulder.

After a moment, she whispered, "We made love, Suzie. Um, maybe I should say we had sex. I don't think there was any love."

"Shit."

"Yeah."

"You're sure?"

Shelley glanced up. "I'm pretty sure I know about having sex."

"No, I mean, are you sure there was no love in it?"

She couldn't reply to that out loud, but internally, she knew. Yes, there was love in it, at least from her perspective. She'd never stopped loving Matt. Not really.

He obviously didn't feel the same.

Pulling back, Suzie cupped Shelley's face in her hands and tilted it to look straight into her eyes. "Give yourself time. Give him time. Shelley, he's been miserable for years. Hard to turn misery off on a dime."

"No, Suzie." Shelley blinked away tears and shook her head. "It's too late. I told him to forget me and move on. There is too much hurt. Frankly, I'm not worth it. I'm the last person he needs. I'm so screwed up."

Suzie pursed her lips. "You are *not* screwed up. You are emotional. You are confused. You gave into sex when maybe you should have waited but you're not screwed up. And dammit, you *are* worthy."

"Suzie..."

"I don't want to hear any more about that. You hear me? Stop beating yourself up." She stood. "Now, get some sleep. Tomorrow, we play. Shopping first, and then going to pig out on all those leftovers. Then we get to work. Next week is full and I'm relying on your help. Got it? So get yourself a good night's sleep."

Was this her sister's way of keeping her busy so she wouldn't think about Matt? Confused a little at her sister's turn, she said, "Sure, Suzie. It's just...."

Suzie headed for the door, talking over her shoulder. "I mean it, Shell. You don't have *time* to pine away about Matt so snap out of it. We've got work to do."

That was it.

Suzie paused for a second, and then left the room, closing the door behind her. Sighing, Shelley flicked off the bedside light and fell back onto the pillows.

"Snap out of it. Sure. I'll just do that."

Dark blanketed her and she was surprised to realize that her tears were gone, and she didn't feel like crying any more. That was good. At once, her door opened again, a triangle of light pushing through while Suzie poked her head inside the room.

"One question," she said.

"Okay."

"Was it good?"

No hesitation. "It was wonderful."

"Then that's all I need to know." Click.

The door closed and the dark was back. *Thank God.*

~

Matt could have spent the night with his mother, sisters, and the kids, but opted to head back up the mountain. According to the road crews, the mountain road was passable, but he still had to be cautious. He took his time, letting his mind drift a little about the past twenty-four hours or so, even though he had to pay close attention to his driving.

He'd become comfortable with his self-pity. That was a fact. The comfort lay in the fact that it was safe. He shook his head at the thought. What had he become? He'd been a bit of a risk-taker in his youth and now it seemed that a woman had turned him into a man who lived in a safety net.

Not that safety wasn't a bad thing. Hell, he was a cop. He was supposed to be all about safety—keeping the town's residents safe, making sure drivers followed the rules, teaching street safety to kids at the elementary school.

Naw, that wasn't what he was talking about. He was living the safe life. Not putting himself out there anymore with women to keep himself safe emotionally. And yeah, he was wallowing in his self-pity and pining after a woman who had set him free—not just last night, but years ago.

Shelley *had* set him free and instead of dealing with it and trying to move forward, he'd stuck himself somewhere at the crossroads of pity and longing—longing for something, or someone, he was never going to have again.

No more.

His mother was right. He deserved to be happy.

His resolve remained high the last few miles to this cabin but once inside the doors of his home, he was immediately taken with the lingering scent of Shelley and the remnants of their night spent together in front of the fire—blankets scattered, ottoman pushed back, the clothes of his she wore in a heap by the sofa.

Empty. The place where he'd carved out his safe existence suddenly felt empty without her—even after one night.

He rounded the furniture and sat on the ottoman, staring at the place where they had made love. His heart raced, recalling how he'd felt. How she felt in his arms. How perfectly happy he had been with her for that one, beautiful, night.

Propping his elbows on his knees, he raked his fingers

through his hair, his head hanging. Dammit. He loved her still. How was he going to do this? Do what he told his mother?

How as he going to figure out how to live without her, while still loving her with all his heart?

Chapter Twelve

"Okay, so here is the deal. I've dropped the kids off at Mama and Daddy's so you, my dear sister, are coming to the lodge with Brad and me. It is, after all, New Year's Eve."

Shelley looked up from the book she was reading and took in her sister's stern expression. "I thought I was babysitting."

"No. Change of plans."

"But I wanted to babysit."

Suzie stood hands on hips, her stance broad, her barely five-foot-three frame erect, her look determined. They'd been through this no less than a dozen times already. Brad was hosting a big New Year's Eve bash at the lodge, the first one in a couple of decades or more. With the renovation finished, he had invited the entire town for a New Year's celebration.

Suzie wanted Shelley to go.

Shelley wanted none of it.

Babysitting was her excuse.

"You've worked your fingers to the bone all week trying to forget about Matt. You've brooded long enough. You're going to get out and party tonight."

She fiddled with a page of the book. "I'm not brooding. I've already told you. I'm not going."

"You're a stubborn little minx."

She returned to her reading. "No more stubborn than you. Besides, now that I'm not babysitting, I can finish this book."

Plopping beside her on the couch, Suzie grasped the book and pushed it into Shelley's lap. "You can read anytime. It's New Year's Eve. That only comes once a year. Come on, sis. Let your hair down."

Snorting, she shifted on the couch. "I don't need to let my hair down. My hair is fine. My life is fine. I want to stay here and read." She snatched up her book and turned a page. "Besides, as soon as tomorrow is over, I need to start moving the kids and me into the lodge, so I should probably pack a few things. And plan. Since I don't have a car now, I need to figure that out too. I just have stuff to do, Suzie, so I'll stay here."

Suzie huffed. "You can't stay cooped up here forever. You've got to get back into the Harbor Falls social life sooner or later."

"I choose later." She didn't look up. "Besides, I've only been here a week. Give me a break. I don't need to start the new year with back-stabbing whispers about me being the town slut."

"You're not the town slut. I'm pretty sure Candy Crane has that title all tied up. Besides, it's a party! It will put a smile on that sourpuss face of yours."

Not liking that last comment, she glared at her sister. "I do not have a sourpuss face."

"You do."

"Not."

"Do."

"Not! Crap. I'm not arguing with you!"

"I bought a dress today. I think you should try it on."

Nice twist, sis. "No. Me and my sourpuss face are having a night in. I'm looking forward to popcorn. Maybe a bubble bath. Mind if I use your tub?"

Rising, Suzie looked down at her. "You can be so damn difficult."

Smiling into her book, Shelley replied, "I know. I like to get my way."

"All right. You've got it." Heading toward the kitchen, she called over her shoulder. "I'm going to leave the dress on my bed, in case you change your mind after you take that bubble bath."

Shelley listened for her fading footsteps.

"Not freakin' likely," she muttered, her nose stuck further in her book.

~

Matt stepped onto his mother's porch and twisted the door handle to let himself in. "Mom? I'm here," he called into the room. "You ready?"

She called out from the back of the house. "Almost. Be right there."

He paused at the entry and looked at himself in the antique hall tree mirror. Adjusting his tie, he loosened it a bit, pulling it away from his neck. "Damn tie," he muttered. "I would only do this for you, you know."

"What?" His mother stepped beside him.

"I said I would only do this for you. I still can't believe you talked me into it." She looked stunning standing there beside him. "By the way, you look beautiful. Papa was a lucky man."

She smiled at his reflection and straightened his tie. "You're looking pretty spiffy yourself. And you're right, your Papa *was* a lucky man."

Grinning into the mirror, he caught the sparkle in her eye.

"Do you good to get out, Matthew. Holed up there in that cave of yours," she said. "You need to come out and play once in a while."

He snorted. "I'm not a social butterfly like my sisters. You know that. But I'm working on it."

Shrugging, she smiled again. "Ah, but you don't have to be the social bug. Just be you. That's good enough."

She grasped his shoulders and turned him to face her. "Matthew Branson, I'm going to say something that I never thought I would say. Son, you need a woman."

Heat flushed his cheeks and neck. "Mom, don't go there."

She narrowed her gaze. "Matthew, what is it you want in life? You worry the hell out of me."

He never meant to worry her. Never had. He loved her with everything that was in him. "All I ever wanted was what you and Papa had. A home, a family..."

"A wife."

"Yes."

"Shelley?"

He paused. "Once upon a time."

Squinting at him, she went on. "You won't find a wife, or make amends with Shelley, moping around in that cabin of yours."

He studied his shoes. "No, ma'am, I suppose I won't." Having a conversation about Shelley was the last thing he wanted to do tonight. "But let's get things clear, making amends with Shelley is never going to happen. So, give me time on finding someone new. I can't just turn off loving her like that."

Crooking her finger under his chin, she lifted his face. "Son," she began softly, "and you're never going to. Let the past go. Make her yours. Before it's too late."

Staring into his mother's eyes, he sensed the unspoken words. She'd lost her love, his Papa, way too early.

"There are no guarantees, ever. All you have is today. Don't waste it."

He swallowed hard, knowing it was already too late, but he nodded and smiled at his mom. "I'll work on it," was all he said, knowing it was a lame promise.

"Do that," she told him. "A lot of time has already gone by. Don't dismiss the time you do have. You won't regret it."

With bubbles up to her ears, Shelley sank into Suzie's whirlpool tub, leaned back with her book, and toed the lever to turn off the water. Letting loose of a long sigh, she delighted in the hot water and the steady beat of the jets against her tired muscles. They'd had a long week and had worked hard. In a couple of days, she would move into the lodge with the girls, so more work was headed her way. Tonight, now that she was off kid duty, all she wanted was to relax.

She soaked until the water grew tepid, the bubbles gone, and the book finished. The bathroom was chilly, so she dried quickly and wrapped herself in a thick towel. The inn had the best towels, Suzie didn't skimp on that. Rarely did she skimp on anything. The soft terry felt good against her skin. Hurrying through Suzie's bedroom toward her own, she stopped abruptly at the bed and stared at the simple black dress that lay across it.

Chapter Thirteen

The lodge was full of people, and well, people weren't his thing. Of course. Matt slipped out a French door leading out onto the deck and braved the winter cold. The deck was cleared of snow, thankfully, so he didn't have to worry about slipping. The lake sat like a giant jewel beyond the lodge, moonlight flickering off its icy depths. He moved to the rail, peered out into the night, and exhaled.

"Sometimes crowds get to me, too."

Matt looked to his left while Brad Matthews stepped closer. "Yeah. I'm not much for parties." Then thinking better of that statement, he added, "But as far as parties go, this is a great one. My mother is having a wonderful time."

Brad chuckled. "I love to entertain but I've been prepping for this for days. I needed a break." He glanced to the lake. "Man, I am so glad I didn't tear this place down."

Matt agreed. "Me, too. I sure was sweating it with my cabin a mile up the road. I'm glad you left it as is."

"Well, if it hadn't been for Suzie's stubbornness, it probably wouldn't have happened."

"Must run in the family."

"Stubbornness?"

"Um. Yeah."

"I hear that goes two ways."

Matt's gaze landed on Brad's face and he wondered what he meant. Well, of course, Shelley had probably talked with Suzie, and Suzie had discussed with her husband. There was no time to ponder that notion, however, when the French door cracked open again behind them and the commotion inside spilled out onto the deck.

A sequined Suzie squeezed through the door.

"There you are!" She sidled up next to Brad and smiled. "Hi, Matt. It's so good to see you here." She turned her attention to her husband. "Honey, a couple of heat cans under the serving dishes have gone out and I can't find any more. Where do you keep them? Oh, and we are out of pâté. You know how Claire Harper loves her pâté..."

Rolling his eyes, Brad patted her arm. "I'll take care of it," then turning to Matt, he added, "See you later man, glad you're here. Hey, there could be a poker game later tonight if you want to stick around."

Matt nodded and Brad was gone.

Suzie faced him. "It *is* good to see you, Matt. It's been a while and I wish we could see each other more often. I sort of miss the old days when... Oh!" Reaching to her waist, she pulled a cell phone from her skirt waistband. "On vibration. Just a sec. Could be the kids." She swiped at the phone and he waited while she said things like "um-huh," and "yes, of course," and "you're sure?" and then finally, "see you in a few." She ended the call, slipped the phone back in her waistband, exhaled long, bit her lip and then squared her gaze on him.

"Matt Branson, I need your help. I know you are here for the party and I hate to take you way from it but... Oh, Lord, I really need some help."

Concerned now, he wondered if this was a police matter. "What is it, Suzie? Is there trouble?"

Her brow knit and she paused. "Not sure. Yes, maybe. Yes. There is trouble. At my house. Someone is sneaking around outside. Strange noises too, Shelley said, and..."

Panic raced to his throat, constricting his breath. *No.*

"I'm just not exactly sure what kind of trouble there could be, but Shelley said the lights were flickering and she wondered if the man outside had—"

Matt grasped her forearms. "No problem. I'm on my way." He turned away from Suzie and jerked open the French door to the dining area. "Tell Shelley I'm coming. Tell my mother I..." he shouted over his shoulder. "Just tell her I'm going after what I need to go after."

"Shelley?"

"Yes!"

"Go Matt go!"

≈

The dress fit like a glove. Sleek and black, the length hit above the knee, the plunging neckline showed a comfortable amount of cleavage, the three-quarter length sleeves skimmed her forearms.

Shelley turned and looked at herself in the mirror from all angles. Suzie was right. The dress was perfect. Too bad she didn't have the guts to wear it out in the light of day.

Or to a New Year's Eve bash.

After her bath, she couldn't resist trying it on. She found it difficult to stop at just wearing the dress, though. She donned pantyhose and found a pair of Suzie's black pumps. Getting into the dress-up thing, she rummaged through her sister's jewelry and found a very nice pearl necklace with matching earrings. Oh, and a nice diamond tennis bracelet.

"Might as well put on a little makeup," she mused, stepping back from the mirror.

In fifteen minutes, she was dressed, fluffed, decked out, spit-shined, and polished.

"All dressed up and nowhere to go."

Staring at herself, she wondered... Did she dare? Before she could back out, she picked up her phone and called her sister.

"Talk me out of this," she said, "I think I want to come to the party."

"Um-huh."

"Can you come get me?"

"Yes, of course," Suzie replied.

"Okay." Her heart skipped a beat. Would she really do this?

"You're sure?"

"Yes."

"See you in a few."

They hung up. Shelley bit her lip and stared at her reflection. "Shit. I'm going to a party."

His heart pounding, Matt spun his tires as he rounded the corner and sped into Suzie's driveway. Running the Jeep almost up to the doorstep, he haphazardly parked the vehicle, left it running, and jogged up the sidewalk and onto the porch. Repeatedly, he jammed the heel of his hand on the doorbell.

"Answer the door, Shelley. Answer the door."

Impatient, he shifted from one foot to another. It wasn't until the door jerked open that he realized the lights were on in the house.

"I'm coming! Geez, Suze." Shelley's voice trailed off as the door swung fully open. Her jaw dropped. "M-Matt?"

He pushed his way inside. "Close the door. Tell me what you saw."

She wrinkled her brow. "What?"

"You called. Suzie said you saw someone messing around the house. Where was he? In the front or back by the lake? What did you see?" He knew his voice was frantic. Why was she standing there so calm? And why was she so dressed up?

"Matt, I didn't see anyone messing around. I called Suzie to come and take me to the lodge."

Realization hit him. He stepped back, distancing himself from Shelley. "What?"

"I didn't call Suzie about a man, Matt. I called her to come pick me up."

"Hell fire." Raking his fingers through his hair, he paced away and then turned back toward her. He couldn't do anything but stare. "Shit. And goddamn, you look so, freaking, hot. I mean, beautiful." Finally, he sat with a thud on the sofa, his elbows on his knees, his head in his hands, staring at the floor. "Shit."

Shelley stepped toward him. "Matt, calm down. I'm okay. This is..."

"This is a set-up," he told her, looking up into her face. *Dammit.*

"I don't understand."

"You called. I was there standing by Suzie. She said there was trouble here at the house, someone messing around, and that... Hell, never mind. You get it, right?"

Shelley huffed out a breath and rolled her eyes. "Oh my God. My sister! Matt Branson, if you think I had anything to do with this, you're wrong. My sister has been playing matchmaker. I did *not* call to have you come get me."

Neither of them said anything. Matt washed his hands over his face and stared at the floor again. After a moment, Shelley moved to the couch and sat down beside him.

He looked at her. "I thought my heart was going to jump out of my chest I was so worried about you."

Shelley nodded. "I could tell you were upset."

"Dammit, Shelley, I'm a mess. I thought you were in trouble."

Sighing, she touched his hand. "Thank you for caring, Matt."

"I never stopped caring, Shelley.

She smiled. "We're a pair, aren't we?" She stared straight ahead into the Christmas tree lights.

"Yeah." He lowered his hands. He studied her profile. The twinkle of the Christmas lights reflected against her soft skin.

"Matt," she whispered, "I lied."

His heart rate kicked up a notch. "About what?"

She faced him. "I don't want you to forget me. I don't want you to move on. I don't want to let you go. I want... a chance." Her gaze fell to her lap and she fiddled with the hem of the dress.

"Shelley..."

She shook her head. "No, please don't stop me. Let me say this while I can. I know I hurt you. I know you don't like me very much. And I know there is this big chunk of history that we have to get over. But I can't get you out of my head, and I can't ever forget how much I loved you once upon a time. Beyond that, I ache every minute of the day knowing that I hurt you so damn much and that you are still hurting." She took a deep breath and exhaled. It was then he noticed the tear trailing down her cheek. "The thing is, I don't know what I can do to make it better. I've apologized. You still hate me. I don't know how to fix this."

Closing his eyes, Matt swallowed and gathered his wits about him. His mother's words rang in his ears. "I don't hate you," he whispered. Turning, he placed his hands on both her shoulders and turned her to face him. "I know how to fix it."

Her eyes brimmed with tears. "How?"

"I need to let the past go."

"I need to think there could be a future."

He slipped the tear away with his forefinger. "Just love me. The rest will come."

"I've never stopped loving you, Matt."

Grasping a tendril of her hair, he twisted it around his forefinger and pulled her closer. As his lips moved in to capture hers, he whispered, "I have loved you every day of my life, Shelley Hart. Every. Single. Day."

He kissed her. She tasted like home—like a million years of wandering, finally settling in the place of his dreams. Pulling away, he peered into her eyes.

"We need time."

She nodded. "And lots of talk."

His gaze dropped to her lips. "And kissing?"

Leaning forward, she lightly touched hers to his again. "Yes. Kissing may help." Her gaze played over his face. "And making love?"

He growled and nuzzled her neck.

"Matt, more than anything, I want us to try again. I'll do anything..."

Wrapping her up in his arms, he held her close. "All you have to do is love me," he breathed, "and let me take you home."

Home. Where he should have taken her all those years ago.

"That's easy," she whispered back. "Home is the only place I want to be."

A Note from Maddie

Friends,

Did you enjoy reading *Take My Heart*?

I have to admit two things: the first, I cried when I wrote the scene where Shelley showed up on Suzie's porch, and second, my heart literally pounded when Matt and Shelley finally got back together. Happy endings abound!

If you enjoyed reading Shelley and Matt's story, then please consider sharing with others. One of the best ways to tell others about the book is to leave a review at Goodreads, or at the bookstore where you purchased the book. You can also leave reviews at my website, maddiejamesbooks.com.

Ready for more Sweet Hart Inn? Scroll on to read the first chapter of the next story, *Match My Heart.*

Match My Heart

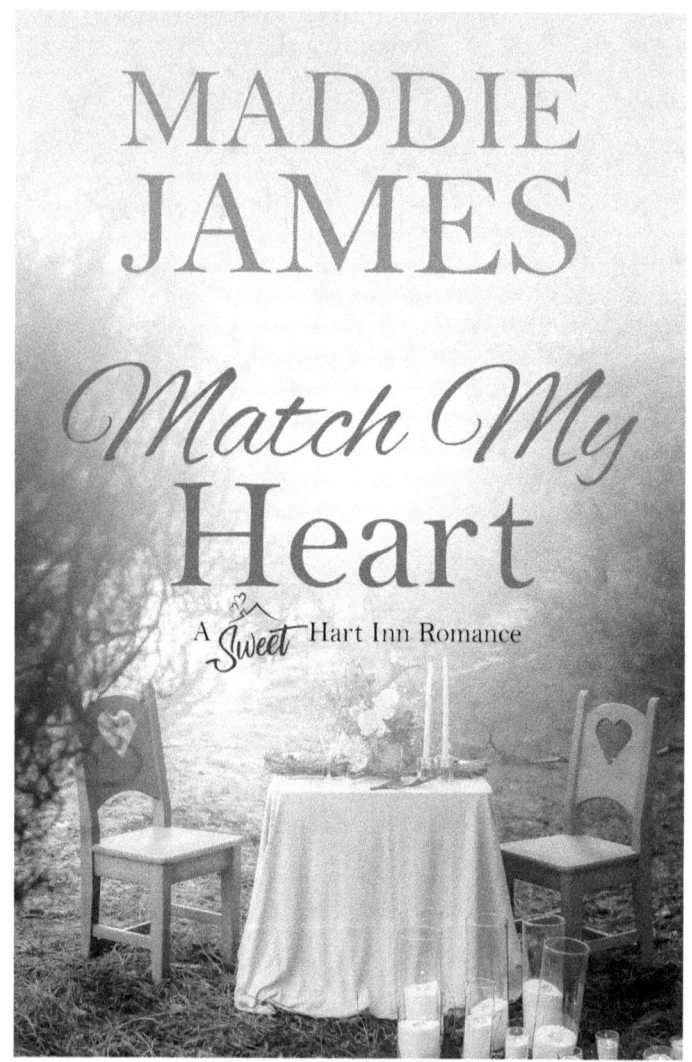

MADDIE JAMES

Match My Heart

A *Sweet* Hart Inn Romance

Match My Heart Sample

Chapter One

The sushi looked fabulous.

Suzie Hart-Matthews glanced up at the smiling Japanese girl behind the counter rolling rice, spicy tuna and seaweed, and shrugged. "Who would have thought that Ralph's Grocery would ever hire a sushi girl?"

The young woman smiled back and said, "See what you want? I make more."

Shaking her head, Suzie returned, "Oh no. You've quite a selection here." She reminded herself to tell her husband, Brad, about her new discovery. The two of them being chefs, they were always interested in the new food offerings in their small town of Harbor Falls.

Somehow, though, she couldn't imagine sushi on the menu at Falls Lodge, Brad's business. Nor could she imagine it at Sweet Hart Inn. Even though breakfast was the norm at her inn, occasionally she hosted dinner parties or events. Sushi on the menu in this Blue Ridge mountain town seemed, well, a little out of place. Yet, intriguing.

She picked up a pretty salmon roll—it looked and smelled fresh—and slipped it into her grocery cart.

A deep voice came from behind her. "What do you think of my sushi bar, Suzie?"

Suzie turned to face Ralph Myers, owner of the grocery. Rumor had it he bought out his business partner and was going independent. Recently, he'd been trying a lot of new twists to get Harbor Falls residents to buy their groceries local rather than driving to one of the big box stores in the next county. Keeping business local was of prime concern to the residents and small business owners here.

Hence, the sushi attempt.

Glancing at the display again, she said, "The sushi looks great, Ralph. But whatever possessed you?"

He cut her off with a wave of both hands and leaned her way. "Did you meet my new sushi chef? I stole her from a restaurant in Charlotte, temporarily, to see how it works out. Just the thing Harbor Falls needs." Then he proudly stepped back and crossed both arms over his chest while nodding. "We're uptown now."

How can you doubt a man who is so pleased with himself? "I hope it works out, Ralph." She glanced toward the meat counter. "Now, tell me about your beef sale. I need a couple of nice juicy ribeyes."

He led her to the counter and proceeded to tell Bart Shackler behind it to get her a couple of extra-thick cuts, the best he had.

"Now, Ralph," she batted her eyes, "y'all don't have to give me special treatment."

He bowed and swept a hand in front him. "Ma'am, yes I do. If I keep you buying from me, Ms. Famous Cookbook Author, I can claim you as my own customer. See?" He pointed to the wall beside of the meat case.

Suzie cast her gaze on the wall there. "Well, knock me over with a noodle. Ralph, what in the world have you done?"

A huge poster graced the wall. On it was a picture of her—the same photograph on her just-released cookbook, *Best of Sweet Hart Inn*—with a tag line that read, *Harbor Falls' Celebrity Chef, Suzie Hart, Shops at Ralph's!*

"Oh my! Ralph, you shouldn't have done that!" She was embarrassed to say the least, but not one bit surprised that Ralph would try to capitalize on her recent success. At least he got her name right on the poster. She had chosen to stay Suzie Hart professionally, in her cookbook world. Still, she was homegrown Harbor Falls and while she was flattered, it made her uncomfortable. But she guessed it was fine with her—as long as that was as far as it went.

Ralph leaned and winked. "Hope you don't mind, Suzie. I'll give you ten percent off your order if you let me keep it up. I'd like to put an ad in the paper, too."

Now that made her a mite uncomfortable. She smiled sweetly. "Ralph Myers, I've shopped your store all my life and I have no intention of shopping anywhere else. I'm honored to have my poster up in your store and you can keep your ten percent, because," she reached out and grasped his hand and leaned forward herself, "that's the way we do things here in Harbor Falls." She smiled and then added, "Oh, but before you put that in the paper, we will need to get permission from the publisher to use that photo." She bit her lip and gave him a frown. "Sorry to say sometimes these things take time. Let me work on that, okay?"

Ralph's smile turned frown-like as well. "I didn't think of that. Do you mind taking care of it?"

She didn't. Suzie also knew that the likelihood they would agree would be zero-to-none. Her publisher was mighty hands-on and picky with publicity so this could truly take a while—or not happen at all. She didn't mind the national publicity she'd recently enjoyed for her cookbook, but the local hype was a little embarrassing. In Harbor Falls, she just wanted to be Suzie, detached of the celebrity persona.

He covered her hand with his and nodded—in gratitude, she suspected. Then he left her and headed toward the front of the store, tossing a hand up at another customer coming down the aisle.

Sighing, Suzie looked back at the poster. "Oh boy," she said under her breath. "Brad will get a kick out of this." She pulled out her cell phone and snapped a quick picture of the poster.

Movement to her right caught her attention as someone else stepped up to the meat counter. Mary Lou Picketts stood staring at the wall, too. *Oh dear, what will the rest of Harbor Falls think of this?* Again, she was a tad embarrassed.

She followed Mary Lou's gape, however, and realized that she wasn't exactly looking at the Suzie poster, but that something else had caught the young woman's eye.

A different kind of sigh exited Mary Lou's lips. Suzie watched as the young woman gazed up at another poster of a man, lean, dark and gritty, standing with a guitar slung over his shoulder. Suzie studied her side profile as Mary Lou took in the full-color and full-body likeness of Nash Rhodes, Nashville's newest up-and-coming country music star.

Adoration. That was the look on Mary Lou's face.

No, that wasn't it.

Adolescent crush-like puppy love?

Good God no. Mary Lou had to be close to thirty and was way past the adolescent crush phase of her life. The look was something else. Like staring at something just out of reach. Perhaps lost and given up on.

Longing?

Love?

Suzie shook her head. Of course not. No one falls in love

with a celebrity icon. Oh, they may *think* they are in love, but how could they truly be? You cannot fall in love with someone by reading their fanzines, watching them on CMT, scouring the Internet for tidbits of information, and going to their concerts.

Longing. Maybe it was more like longing.

Suzie thought about that. Mary Lou lived a quiet and perhaps slightly isolated life here in Harbor Falls. Suzie had known her since grade school, even though Mary Lou was a few years younger. Still, everyone knew everyone in Harbor Falls, pretty much. Mary Lou was the type of girl who never really had a best girlfriend and kept to herself most of the time. Suzie seemed to remember that she did go off to college—but she wasn't quite certain what Mary Lou had done with her life since then. She'd heard she worked from home, but at what, Suzie didn't know.

Mary Lou heaved another sigh. Suzie watched her chest rise, her breasts lift, and then fall in a half-defeated motion. She felt a little sorry for her and wasn't quite sure why.

Suzie took a few steps and leaned Mary Lou's way. "Hard to believe he's going to be in Harbor Falls next weekend, isn't it?" The poster advertised the benefit concert to raise money for the children's wing of the hospital. Nash was the star attraction but there was a local act opening Nash's performance. Suzie's husband, Brad, who was on the hospital board, had a big hand in bringing Nash to their small town, so she had some personal scoop on the musician and his appearance.

The young woman swung her way and jumped back a little. "Oh! Suzie. I didn't know anyone was there!"

Smiling, Suzie reached out to grasp her elbow. "No problem, honey. Didn't mean to startle you. Thought I'd say hello. Came in to pick up some meat."

Mary Lou rotated her gaze back toward the poster. "Yeah. Meat. A hunk of it."

"Mary Lou!" Suzie chuckled.

Her hands fluttered to her neck. "Oh! Did I say that out loud?"

"Sure enough did, sweetie." Suzie stepped up beside her and they stood and ogled the poster together. "I do have to agree that the man is definitely one prime choice of—"

"Beefsteak?"

The women rolled their gazes toward the meat case and Bart who was holding out Suzie's ribeyes.

"Ahem. Yes. Thanks, Bart."

"No problem, dear." A sly grin broke his lips and he retreated.

Suzie grabbed her steaks and gave Mary Lou a smile as she turned to set them in her cart. Mary Lou waved as she headed in a brisk walk toward the bakery.

But Suzie couldn't stop thinking about the look on Mary Lou's face and how discontented that sigh sounded earlier that came from her lips.

Still watching, Suzie took stock. Her clothes were rather baggy, but underneath, her frame was small with rounded hips moving beneath the jogging pants. Mary Lou turned and Suzie caught site of a rounded contour in the chest area.

Mary Lou Picketts was hiding a rack under those old baggy clothes!

Moving to her face, devoid of make-up, Suzie took stock of a smooth, peaches and cream complexion hiding behind a mousy brown ponytail caught high on her head, which hung down to frame part of her face.

An interesting notion was growing in Suzie's heart and gut. She glanced once more at the poster of Nash Rhodes, and then back to Mary Lou. Nash *was* doing that big benefit concert at the lodge, and her husband Brad *was* hosting the thing.

Did she dare?

Yes. Consider it a gift to humanity. Besides, she had managed to hook her sister Shelley, and her high school boyfriend, Matt Branson, back up again, hadn't she? That was a rematch made in Heaven. Maybe she could work a little matchmaking magic on Mary Lou.

Lord knows, the girl could stand a break.

Determined, she gripped the cart handle and ventured forth.

"Mary Lou? Wait!"

~

Several hours later, Suzie stood in her kitchen facing her husband. Obviously, he was not drinking the Kool-Aid she was handing him.

"No. Absolutely not," he told her.

"It's just dinner, Brad. It's the least we can do. Besides, it would probably be the one high point in Mary Lou's life. Can't we make a dream come true?"

"As much as I would like to, Suzie, it's impossible." Her husband stared at her. No, glared was more like it.

"Relax, Brad." She stepped forward and smoothed her hands over his muscled chest. "This will not be a problem, I promise you. It's just a quiet dinner here at the inn. No muss no fuss. Please?"

"Out of the question. Nash's people have spelled out exactly what he will, and what he cannot do, while he is in town."

Suzie picked at a piece of lint on his shoulder. "Oh pooh. The boy needs a home cooked meal occasionally, right? He's country through and through and we're just small town. He'd probably welcome it. Why don't you reach out and see if you can make it happen. After all," she sidled in closer and slipped her hands around his waist, "you can be very convincing."

"As can you." He frowned. "This is above and beyond the call of husbandly duties, Suzette."

With a wicked smile, she slipped a couple of fingers under his belt. "I'll repay you later by going above and beyond the call of wifely duties, husband."

Brad groaned and grasped her about the waist.

She continued, "All you need to do is wrangle him away from the lodge for a couple of hours, either before or after the show, and I'll do the rest."

Brad stopped her hands at his waistband by placing his big paws over hers. Those dark eyes of his, always so mesmerizing, peered down. "Not happening. I have no control over his agenda once he gets here. He'll be sequestered away in his bus most of the time, whisked in for the concert, and then back out again. It's a benefit, one that wasn't on their books and they aren't making any money on this—Nash Rhodes is not going to be lingering in Harbor Falls long and I'm not asking for special favors. Especially for some lovelorn wallflower."

Suzie dropped her hands and frowned. "Mary Lou is a very pretty girl under all that hair and fabric. She just lacks confidence and needs a little coaching."

"Whatever. Still, I can't do this."

"He's not staying at the lodge?"

"No. He's parking his bus behind it and staying there."

"Crap. That was my Plan B." She batted her eyes again. Thinking. "Could you get him here a day early, perhaps? Some sort of pre-concert event?"

He grasped her face in his hands. "You persistent little minx. No. The way his manager talks, he's practically on 24/7 call."

"But I bet you could arrange it. Give him the presidential suite and all the amenities you can muster. I'll bake and have a ton of goodies there. I hear he has a sweet tooth. I can't work magic in that trailer of his. I need to get him out of it."

"My dear wife... I love you to pieces, but I am having no part of what you are planning. The man is the current young gun of Nashville. Their shooting star. They've got him booked so tight he doesn't have time to call his mother without being scheduled."

Leaning up on her tiptoes, Suzie smiled and kissed her husband's salty lips, not to be discouraged so easily. "I'm counting on you, Brad Matthews," she whispered. "Did I tell you about the pink furry handcuffs I bought in Asheville the other day? And that strawberry flavored massage gel?"

The groan came from deeper in his chest this time.

"Now go call and see what you can do."

Learn more about *Match My Heart* on my website, or purchase at your favorite bookstore.

Mary Lou and Nash

HARBOR FALLS ROMANCE: SWEET HART INN

Match My
HEART

MADDIE JAMES

More Sweet Heart Inn

Cozy up at the inn where the heart of the Blue Ridge beats strongest...

Welcome to Sweet Hart Inn, a charming bed and breakfast nestled along the peaceful shores of Falls Lake, at the foot of Falls Mountain. At the center of it all is chef and innkeeper Suzie Hart, whose kitchen is always warm, and whose heart is always open. Together with her husband Brad, Suzie serves up matchmaking advice and comfort food, along with second chances, and a generous helping of happily ever after.

The Sweet Hart Inn Books

All of My Heart
Take My Heart
Match My Heart
Tame My Heart
The Dating Game
Miss Matched Hearts
The Husband List
Chase My Heart
No Sweeter Match
One More Kiss

The Falls Mountain Books

Welcome to Falls Mountain, and the quaint town of Harbor Falls.

Tucked deep into the Blue Ridge Mountains, bricked streets, lakeside views, and charming local shops set the scene for small town romance.

In this standalone-but-interconnected series, you'll meet bakers, bookstore owners, chocolatiers, school teachers, and more—all trying to run their businesses, chase their dreams, and keep their hearts in check. But in Harbor Falls, love has a habit of showing up unannounced...

From second chances to secret babies to grumpy-sunshine pairings, each book brings a satisfying happily-ever-after and a cast of characters you'll want to visit again and again.

Falls Mountain Romance is a companion series to the Sweet Hart Inn Romance books by Maddie James.

Dance into My Heart
The Christmas Nanny
The Heartbreaker

Star Crossed
Not This Christmas
Convince My Heart

I hope you'll check out these books, and my other series, on my website at:
www.maddiejamesbooks.com

About Maddie James

Romance with a pulse—small towns, big love, and a dash of drama.

Maddie James writes small-town romance with heart, heat, and the occasional haunting. Her stories range from sweet to spicy, suspenseful to supernatural—happily-ever-afters guaranteed! From stand-alone love stories to binge-worthy series, Maddie delivers love next door, some cowboy kisses, an occasional hint of danger, and just enough drama to keep things interesting.

Get all the drama delivered to your inbox when you sign-on to Maddie's VIP reader list!

Free books, sneak peaks, bonus content, giveaways, and more...

Learn more: maddiejamesbooks.com/pages/newsletter